The School Pet Who went Missing

DETECTIVE

DOVE

ZUNI BLUE

AMARIA & SARIEL

LONDON

100 Free Gifts For You

There are 100 FREE printables waiting for you!

Certificates, bookmarks, wallpapers and more! You can choose your favourite colour: red, yellow, pink, green, orange, purple or blue.

You don't need money or an email address. Check out www.zuniblue.com to print your free gifts today.

CONTENTS

Case File No.2

In London, England, you'll find Detective Inspector Mya Dove. With four years' experience on the police force, this eight-year-old is on her way to being the best police officer ever.

Yes. The best. Her mum said so.

To inspire other kids, she's sharing case files. Case No.2: The School Pet Who Went Missing.

Chapter 1

"What's twenty-three minus sixteen plus forty-five?" our teacher Mrs Cherry asked. "Anyone know? Anyone at all?"

She looked around the classroom, but no one put their hand up.

"Does anybody know?" Mrs Cherry asked, her face turning as red as her hair. "Anyone want to guess?"

Nope. We didn't care about Maths that day. We were more interested in the big secret at school. No student knew what it was...

"You're being very naughty!" Mrs Cherry threw her hands up and huffed. "If you won't work, you can all sit in silence."

Mrs Cherry took out some homework to mark. Usually she looked bored marking homework, but today she did it with a big smile.

"Um...Miss?" Angel, the meanest girl in school, asked.

"Yes, Angel?"

"Is there anything you want to tell us?"

"…No."

Mrs Cherry grinned. She knew what the big school secret was, but she wouldn't tell us. I guess keeping the secret was punishment for not answering her Maths questions.

While Mrs Cherry marked homework, our class whispered to each other.

"What's the secret?" Emma whispered. "Anyone know?"

"Not me," Ahmarri said quietly.

"Dunno either," Liam said.

"Jimmy," I whispered to my friend. He worked with the Children's Police Force like me. "Any news?"

"Yep! My secret source told me it isn't a big secret, but a *small* one." He stopped to scratch an itchy, red spot on his white cheek. "I don't get it, Mya! What could a SMALL secret be?"

A small secret? It didn't make sense to me either. Nobody keeps a small secret. Big secrets are exciting!

"Only Miss knows the secret," I said. "Maybe someone should ask her what the secret is?"

Everyone was too nervous to ask. I didn't want to either. We were scared of being told off, especially after not doing our Maths questions.

"You scaredy-cats," Angel spat. "I'll do it!"

Angel was mean, but right now she was being very brave. She put her hand up.

"Miss," Angel said, "I heard there's a big secret."

"There is no big secret." Mrs Cherry kept her eyes on the homework spread across her desk. "However, there is a little secret. A *tiny* one."

Everyone leaned in, all eyes shifting from Angel to Mrs Cherry and back.

"Mrs Cherry, my friend said the school bought something for us!"

"So you heard about the little secret? No wonder you naughty children didn't answer my Maths questions. I thought they were just too hard."

"We'd love to do some Maths," Angel said, "but could we talk about the secret first?"

Angel batted her big blue eyes. She always did that when she wanted to get her own way.

"You want to know the secret?" Mrs Cherry asked. "If anyone can guess what the secret is, you'll be the first class to enjoy it."

"Is it a school bus?" someone cried.

Mrs Cherry shook her head.

"Is it a dollhouse with a doll that has blonde hair and blue eyes just like me?" Angel asked, flicking her curls.

Mrs Cherry shook her head again.

"Is it new cricket balls?" Jimmy asked. "New footballs? New basketballs? New tennis balls?"

Mrs Cherry laughed and shook her head again.

Everyone shouted out their guesses. Everyone was wrong. It was so much fun though! I still couldn't believe we were getting another surprise this year. We'd already had so many!

But what was this surprise?

It definitely wasn't a drinking fountain. Our headteacher Mr Badal just bought a new one. The old fountain only had boring, plain water. The new one had warm water, cold water, ice water and fizzy water too!

"Come on, class!" Mrs Cherry cried. "The secret surprise is so much fun. Everyone will want a turn playing with it. Mya, any idea what the surprise may be?"

"Just a minute!" I said, my mind racing. I was trying to think of fun surprises. Besides P.E., art and crafts, music lessons and breaktime, school wasn't really "fun". Not fun like playing video games or dressing up dolls. It was hard to think of doing something fun at school.

"Mrs Cherry," I said, "is the surprise another trampoline?"

"You wish!" She laughed. "One trampoline is more than enough."

A new trampoline was the last "fun" surprise we got at school. It wasn't like the tiny one we had before. This one could take two kids at once, even though that's dangerous. They might bounce up high and bang into each other! Ouch!

"Last chance to guess," Mrs Cherry said. "It'll be breaktime any second now. Maybe another class will guess first…Do you give up?"

Everyone nodded.

After the new drinking fountain and trampoline, nobody had expected another good surprise so soon. Usually school surprises were bad like a surprise test. I hated not being able to study first!

Mrs Cherry rushed to the classroom door and peeked outside. Then she put a finger to her lips and crept back to her desk.

"I shouldn't be doing this," she said quietly, "but I think our class deserves the surprise, despite your naughtiness today…"

If Mrs Cherry was breaking the rules then she really, REALLY wanted this surprise too. We all crept over to her desk while she searched through her bags.

"Stay very quiet," she said. "Somehow in all that racket it's gone to sleep."

Sleep? I thought to myself. Is the surprise *alive?*

Mrs Cherry reached under her desk and pulled out a cage. Inside was a water bottle attached to a short, metal tube. Half the water had gone, so the secret had to be very thirsty.

Next to the water bottle was a small bowl of dried fruit and nuts. Close by were tiny stairs leading to an area covered in wood shavings. On the shavings was a plastic container with a tiny hole for a door.

Inside the container was a tiny hamster. It was asleep on a pile of fluffy, cotton wool. It was the cutest hamster in the entire world, and it was ours. So tiny, so soft. We all got a turn stroking it gently.

When I touched it, it opened one eye and looked at me. I looked at it. I knew we'd be great friends. As my gran would say, I could just feel it in my bones.

"Is it a pretty girl like me or a boy?" Angel asked, twirling her curly blonde hair around her finger.

"Oh dear." Mrs Cherry's cheeks turned bright pink. "I'm ashamed to say I didn't ask whether it's a boy or girl. The hamster's previous owner had a very bad cold, so I didn't stay long enough to ask many questions."

Mrs Cherry took her turn stroking the tiny hamster's soft fur.

"Unfortunately, class, this makes picking a name difficult. We'd better pick one girl's name and one boy's name. When I find out its gender, I will let you all know."

Everyone suggested a name. Some were common names like John and Jane. Others were funny names like Biscuit and Peanut. Someone said we should call it Hamster.

Hamster the hamster? No way!

"Okay, okay…" Mrs Cherry took a deep breath. "Those are all very interesting suggestions, but which one should I pick?" She looked down at the homework she'd been marking. "I know! I'll decide based on who scored top marks for their homework."

Everyone but Angel and I groaned.

"Let's see…" Mrs Cherry looked over the homework. "Interesting…"

"Who did the best?" Angel cried. "I mean, I know *I* did but…"

"I studied so hard!" I said. "I read the textbook five times before answering the questions!"

"Oh boy," Mrs Cherry said. "This is a tough one."

Everyone was silent. Nobody moved. As Mum would say, you could've heard a pin drop. I think it was so quiet, you could've heard a feather drop too.

"The person with the top marks for their homework is—"

The bell rang.

"Oh well," Mrs Cherry said. "We'll wait until after breaktime.

Usually everyone rushed out when the bell rang. Not this time. We had to drag our feet to the door. Nobody wanted to leave our hamster. And everyone wanted to know who the homework winner was.

I hoped it was me!

I didn't want Angel to give our hamster any silly names. I couldn't believe the ones she'd picked. Pink Unicorn Flower? No way! Sparkly Sunshine Princess? Never! The other hamsters would laugh at our hamster in the hamster playground!

If there was a hamster playground…

At playtime, Jimmy and I sat together on a bench. Usually he'd run off to play football, but today he stayed with me. He kept looking up at our classroom window.

"Do you think it's a boy or not?" he asked.

"Dunno," I said. "I'd like another girl in class!"

"No way," he cried. "There's lots already! Another boy might even things up a bit."

"Soon we'll know if it's a girl or boy," I said. "All we have to do is wait…"

It was a very long breaktime. Fifteen minutes felt like forever. Angel and her mean friends gave me angry looks. Jimmy and I gave them angry looks right back.

"If Angel has the top marks, she'll get to name our hamster," Jimmy said. "Her names were HORRIBLE! Did you hear the worst ones?"

I shook my head.

"Peachy Sunflower Rainbow. Pretty Purple Snowflake. Starry Day Cloud. The hamster's gonna be SO embarrassed if we call it any of those weird names."

"Don't worry," I said. "I worked harder than ever on my homework. She didn't get higher marks than me!"

Angel and I both wanted to win this homework battle, but someone was going to lose. Only one of us had the top marks, but who could it be?

Angel thought it was her.

I thought it was me.

We were both wrong…

Chapter 2

"Can we see the hamster, Miss?" Angel asked. "I want to name it."

"Finish your work first."

"But—"

"I said to finish your work first," Mrs Cherry said. "No work, no hamster. Is that clear?"

"Yes, Miss," we all said.

It was hard to focus on the questions and answers. I wanted to play with the hamster again. I could hear it running in its wheel. It was very fit and healthy. Just like my mum.

My mum was a nurse, so being healthy was very important to her. Being sick meant she couldn't be there to help hospital patients.

"Are we all done?" Mrs Cherry asked.

Everyone nodded.

"Good. Close your books. Pens down. Could Angel and Mya come up here, please?"

We hurried to the whiteboard and stood as far apart as we possibly could.

Mrs Cherry picked up the hamster and stood between Angel and me. I think it smiled at me, but I'm not sure…

My big brother Will said hamsters don't smile, but I couldn't trust him. He'd told porkies before. One time he said Santa Claus wasn't real, but that turned out to be a big fat lie. We met Santa at the shopping centre. I got to pet the reindeers, even Rudolph!

Mrs Cherry raised her hand so everyone

stopped talking.

"Class, as I said before, the student who scored the highest marks for their homework will name our school pet."

I crossed my fingers.

No matter what happens, I thought, I tried my hardest and did my very best. I just hope I did better than Angel's best.

"Class, the results are in! Drumroll, please!"

Everyone beat their desks like a drum until Mrs Cherry raised her hand. Then the room was completely silent.

"Let's start with Angel," Mrs Cherry said. "She scored an impressive…nineteen out of twenty."

The whole class clapped for her. I forced myself to clap so I wouldn't be told off.

"Thank you, thank you!" Angel curtsied and wiped fake tears from her eyes. "I'd like to thank my mum, my dad and myself for working so hard. I am going to name the hamster—"

"Wait a minute," Mrs Cherry said. "We haven't heard Mya's result yet."

"Surely she didn't do better than me!" Angel snapped, crossing her arms. "I have the highest IQ in the entire school."

"I doubt you have a higher IQ than the teachers, sweetie," Mrs Cherry said, "but you are correct. Mya did not score more than you."

I didn't want Angel to see me cry. I would fight the tears until I got back to my desk. Then I would bury my face in the textbook and cry like a baby. My friends Jimmy and Libby would see me crying, but they wouldn't laugh at me. Angel would.

"I tried my best," I said sadly.

"Cheer up, Mya," Mrs Cherry said.

"Angel scored nineteen out of twenty, but you scored…"

I held my breath. Nobody moved. Even the hamster froze.

"Nineteen!" Mrs Cherry cried. "You both scored nineteen. It was a tie!"

Mrs Cherry looked happy about it. She was the only one. Angel's face turned dark red. I was a bit angry too, but my face didn't change colour because I'm a black person. We don't change colours like that.

"Because it was a tie, both of you may choose a name."

Mrs Cherry moved to the side. Now she could see Angel and me at the same time. We still kept away from each other.

"Based on the names Angel suggested earlier, I have decided that she may choose girls' names. Mya may choose boys' names. Everyone else will vote for their favourite girls' and boys' names. Is that okay, kids?"

We all nodded.

"Angel, which girl names have you chosen?"

Angel paced up and down the classroom, enjoying the attention. She stopped and sighed dramatically before pacing again. Then she reached out to the hamster, so Mrs Cherry handed it over. Angel tried to look in the hamster's eyes but it kept looking over at me instead.

"Hamster, I, Angel White, name you…"

Angel paused for a whole minute.

"…Angel White!"

"Seriously?" I said. "You picked your own name?"

Mrs Cherry wagged her finger at me, so I quickly apologised.

"I did NOT pick my own name," Angel said. "My full name is Angel White. Her full name will be Angel White the Second. See? They're *not* the same."

"Angel White the Second is a really lovely name," Mrs Cherry said. "I wonder what made you think of it…Do you have any other lovely suggestions?"

"Of course I do!" Angel cried. "Instead of Angel White the Second, we can call her…Angelica. Angela. Angelina. If you want something completely different, Angie."

"Angie sounds cute and fluffy, just like the hamster." Mrs Cherry turned to me. "What boy names do you suggest?"

My mind went blank. I had thought of some names when I was in the playground, but now I'd forgotten them all.

"Let's start from the beginning," Mrs Cherry said. She turned to the alphabet chart on the wall. "Which letter should the name start with?"

I didn't want anything beginning with A. I did not want the hamster to be named after Angel. No way! Maybe the name could start with the letter B? Or C? Or D? I didn't know which letter to pick!

"Um...E? No, maybe K? Or J?"

"M!" Angel shouted. "I like the letter M."

"But—"

"Thank you, Angel," Mrs Cherry said.

Angel turned her pointy nose up at me. I stuck out my tongue.

"Mya!" Mrs Cherry shrieked. "That is very unladylike."

"Sorry, Miss."

It was hard thinking of a name. Everyone was staring at me. I didn't want to choose a name they hated. But I didn't want a name I hated either. And I didn't want a name Angel loved.

I thought of every name starting with the

letter M. Can you guess which name came first?

"Mya," I said.

"That is *not* a boys' name," Angel said with a grin. "Try again."

"Michael? Mark? Martin?"

"People in class have those names," Angel snapped. "Try again…unless you want me to choose for you? I like the name Angelo."

If Angel had her way, the hamster's name would start with "Angel". I'd hate that. Every time we called the hamster, I would think of Angel's mean face.

I wouldn't let her choose the name! It was *my* turn. It wasn't right that she'd get to pick two names. I'd worked hard for that high homework mark and this was my reward. Mine, not hers. She'd had her turn.

But I had to act fast! I could see her mind running through names. She wouldn't take very long. Just long enough for everyone to be looking at her for a minute or two. She loved being the centre of attention.

Then her blue eyes darkened like the deep scary part of the sea. She smiled at me. I knew that look. It was her "Ha ha! I win again!" look.

But not this time.

"Malcolm," I said. "I like the name Malcolm."

Mrs Cherry nodded. "I like it too."

Everyone in class liked the name. Everyone but Angel.

"I wanted Angelo," she mumbled.

"That's nice, dear," Mrs Cherry said. "Anyway, the names are Angie and Malcolm. I'll call my friend, the previous owner, and find out what gender the hamster is."

"I thought you'd called at breaktime!" Angel cried.

"Young lady, I was very busy." Mrs Cherry turned away from Angel. "I'll call my friend at lunchtime, I promise. I just hope she's feeling better by now. She might have the flu…"

Lunchtime was almost two hours away, but at least we'd know the truth soon. Would our hamster be Angie or Malcolm? Angel's name or mine? Would she win or would I?

I looked over at the hamster. It was watching me. I walked over and held out my hand. It ran on to it and curled into a ball. A moment later, it fell asleep.

"I think it likes you," Mrs Cherry said.

I thought so too. It always looked at me. Whenever other people held it, it couldn't wait to be back in my hand. It felt like we were best friends already!

If I was the hamster's favourite person that was a good sign. Maybe the hamster was a boy. Maybe it would be called Malcolm after all.

Maybe. Maybe not…

Two hours later, we went to lunch. Everyone else was so jealous of our class because we got to meet the hamster and name it.

"It's no big deal really," Angel said, flicking her curls. "I've had many pets. Three cats, four dogs, one gerbil, two ponies. A hamster isn't THAT amazing when you think about it."

"Where do you keep them all?" one of her mean friends asked.

"Keep them?" Angel laughed. "They are boring after a while, so I give them away. Then I get a brand new one!"

Angel's family was rich. She got whatever she wanted. My mum said she was a spoilt little girl. If spoilt little girls got their own pony, I wanted to be spoilt too…

Angel said she didn't care about the hamster, but she wouldn't stop talking about it. When I looked around the lunch hall, everyone was talking about the hamster. Even my quiet friend Libby had something to say.

Libby had social anxiety. It meant she was very, very nervous around other people. She was only comfortable talking to Jimmy and me.

I scooted closer to Libby and she moved closer to me. She usually had a blank look on her face, but now she looked a little sad.

"What's wrong?" I asked her.

She whispered in my ear, "I'm worried about the hamster."

"What about him…or her?"

"It sneezed when I held it."

"What's wrong with that?" I asked.

"Nothing, if it was one time. It sneezed

three times in a row."

"I'm sure our hamster is just fine," I said. "Maybe it's allergic to your hand lotion?"

"I don't think hamsters are allergic to baby oil…"

"You never know! Any smell can make people sneeze a lot. Last Christmas, Dad sprayed too much air freshener after my brother used the toilet. The freshener made my grandad sneeze five times straight!"

"So a smell could've made the hamster sneeze?"

"Yeah, it could've smelt your baby oil or…" I looked at her straightened afro hair. "Maybe your hair product has a smell. You use hair grease, right?"

"Yeah."

Hair grease was a thick petroleum jelly. Lots of black people like us used it to keep our coily, afro hair soft, shiny and strong.

"Okay, maybe the hamster smelt the hair grease on your hair? Maybe the smell tickled its nose?"

Libby's eyes lowered to her lap. Her hands were shaking. I took one hand and squeezed it. She squeezed back.

"Mya, I'm scared…"

"Why?" I asked, my heart beating faster. "I told you our hamster is okay."

"I think I know why the hamster sneezed," she whispered. "Mrs Cherry said the hamster's last owner had a bad cold. What if the hamster caught it?"

Libby was very quiet. She noticed things other people missed because she wasn't busy talking.

But Libby was also very sensitive. She worried a lot more than other people.

"Don't worry," I said. "He, or she, is going to be just fine."

"Mya, I hope you're right..."

We finished our lunch and went out to play.

People were still talking about the hamster at playtime. Some kids wanted it to be called Angie. Others wanted it to be called Malcolm.

Angel still wanted the hamster to be named after her.

When the bell finally rang, everyone lined up straight away. The teachers were very surprised about that. Usually no one wanted to put their toys away.

Today was different. We wanted to know whether our hamster was a boy or girl. A Malcolm or Angie.

"Upstairs, everyone," Mrs Cherry said. "I have a very important announcement to make."

Back in class, we all sat down and waited

patiently for Mrs Cherry to speak. I was so nervous my teeth chattered. Then I was so excited my heart beat extra fast.

When Mrs Cherry reached into the cage and picked up the hamster, it sneezed.

"Bless you," Libby whispered, looking nervous. "See, Mya? It's got the cold!"

But I wasn't listening.

All I could do was close my eyes and hope the hamster would be called Malcolm. Not Angie or Angela or anything else Angel wanted.

"Are you ready, class?" Mrs Cherry asked.

This was it. We'd finally know if the hamster was a girl or a boy.

Angel looked back at me and glared. I looked away, holding my head high. I didn't stick out my tongue again. This time I was going to be the better person.

"Class, I hope you had a nice lunch. As

promised, I called the hamster's previous owner and was told the hamster's gender."

We waited in complete silence.

"Now for the moment we've all been waiting for…Drumroll, please!"

Jimmy drummed on his desk for a few seconds and stopped.

"Boys and girls, I would like for you to meet our hamster, who will be called…"

Chapter 3

"Boys and girls," Mrs Cherry said, "I would like for you to meet our hamster, who will be called…Malcolm!"

I couldn't believe it! The fluffiest, cutest hamster in the whole world…and I was the one who'd picked his name.

Everyone but Angel clapped. She started fake crying until Mrs Cherry let her hold Malcolm first. I didn't mind. Every time she held him, his name would remind her of me. Ha ha!

"Class, remember that he belongs to the

WHOLE school, not just us."

"Yes, Mrs Cherry," we all said.

"Malcolm is not like your toys. He is a living, breathing animal who needs love and care just like the rest of us."

Mrs Cherry sneezed, making poor Malcolm jump. "Sorry about that...Where was I?"

Angel put her hand up to speak.

"You were telling us that Malcolm is a lot of hard work," Angel said. "I don't see why his parents couldn't just keep him. My mum and dad wouldn't let me stay at school all the time."

"Thank you, Angel," Mrs Cherry grumbled. "Anyway, it is very important that we take good care of him. Make sure his bottle is refilled daily with fresh water."

"Yes, Miss," we all said.

"Change the wood shavings in his cage on

a regular basis, just in case he pees on them. Ensure his poo droppings are cleaned out too. Put them in the small bin bags provided.

"Yes, Miss."

"Daily, I'll let him run around the class in his big, plastic ball. Malcolm will love the change in scenery!"

Everyone else looked tired just thinking about looking after Malcolm. I wasn't bothered by it. I was excited!

I didn't mind picking up a bit of poo from time to time. Angel would have to do it too. I couldn't wait to see her moan about that!

Mrs Cherry reached under her desk and pulled out Malcolm's huge, bright orange ball. It was the biggest hamster ball I'd ever seen. Miss put him inside and placed the ball on the floor.

Malcolm shot off, running between tables and chairs. If he knocked into someone or something, he just turned around and went a different way. It looked like so much fun in there! I wished I could shrink and jump in with him.

Suddenly he ran towards the classroom door. He bumped into it but couldn't leave. The ball's door was locked tight. Even if he did get out, he was too short to reach the classroom door's handle.

"Class, do not let him run around without his ball. He'll get lost and we may never see him again." Mrs Cherry sneezed. "Oh, I hope I didn't catch that cold…"

Malcolm looked so happy in his ball. He had a spinning wheel in his cage, but it wasn't the same as running around class in his big ball.

Running in his ball took him everywhere. He ran into table legs, real legs, chairs, the bin, cupboards, walls and tried breaking through the classroom door a couple of times, but he couldn't escape.

Or so we thought...

Chapter 4

Malcolm had been with us a week and a day. It was hard to focus on schoolwork with him so close by. Sometimes he grabbed the bars on top of his cage and swung about like a monkey. I wanted to sit and watch him, but I had to pay attention to Mrs Cherry's science lesson instead.

Breaktime was so close, but time went by so slowly. That's life, I guess. Time slows down when you've got something good to look forward to.

I was looking forward to a chocolate treat

I'd bought for Malcolm. Real chocolate could hurt hamsters. Special hamster chocolate was perfectly fine.

My mouth watered just thinking about Malcolm's chocolate treat. It looked like real chocolate. Smelt like it too. I wanted to eat the hamster chocolate, but Mum said it was only for hamsters.

"Mya, are you finished?" Mrs Cherry asked.

I finished my work quickly before she told me off. A good police officer doesn't get into trouble. A good police officer sets a good example to others.

"Class, we will continue the research project tomorrow," Mrs Cherry said. "Enjoy your breaktime. And remember, your break lasts for fifteen minutes, not sixteen. Put everything away—"

"In the last two minutes," we all said.

"Have I told you that before?" She blushed, her bushy, red eyebrows twitching. "All right. See you outside in fifteen minutes. Do not be late."

Everyone else rushed out, even Mrs Cherry. Not me, though. I had a packet of special hamster chocolate treats to surprise Malcolm with.

I went to the hamster cage. It was sitting by the windowsill.

"Malcolm? Guess what I got you?"

I gently knocked the top of the cage. I always knocked because it was polite. Remember, a police officer needs permission before they go into someone else's room or house.

Usually Malcolm would come out of his tiny, plastic bedroom, his pink nose twitching. To freshen up, he'd lick himself clean before tidying his hair. Then he'd run down the stairs and stand on his back legs. I'd wave, and imagine he waved back.

Next, I'd open his bedroom and change the cotton wool bedding. If his water bottle was empty, I'd rinse it out and refill it.

When his wood shavings were a bit stinky, I'd throw them out. Mrs Cherry gave me rubber gloves to collect the poo drops Malcolm left all over the cage. Sometimes he was so lazy he even pooed in his bedroom! Yuck!

But none of that happened today. Malcolm was acting differently.

"Hello, Malcolm," I said as he slowly crawled to me. "How are you today?"

His nose twitched and he sneezed. It was a cute little sneeze.

"Bless you."

I picked him up and gave him a hug. He curled up in a ball and half-closed his eyes.

"You look *very* tired," I said. "Did you just wake up?"

Malcolm sneezed again, his eyes watery.

"I hope you aren't catching Mrs Cherry's cold…Maybe a quick tidy up will make you feel better."

I wanted to change his water, bedding and wood shavings, but today he kept getting in the way. Every time I moved him to a different part of the cage, he crawled back on to my hands for a cuddle.

Out the corner of my eye was his big, orange ball. We weren't allowed to put him inside without Mrs Cherry's permission, but I couldn't clean his cage with him getting in the way.

So, I did something very naughty...

I put him inside the ball and locked the lid. Then I placed the ball on the floor and returned to the cage. I had so much work to do and only ten minutes left!

First, I emptied the water in his bottle and refilled it. He'd been drinking so much! A lot more than usual.

Second, I put on some gloves and changed his bedding and any stinky wood shavings. I put all the smelly stuff in a bin bag and tied it up. It kept the smell inside.

When I was done, I washed my hands. There were a few minutes left before class. Malcolm and I still had time for a chat.

"Malcolm, come here," I said.

I waited for the sound of him rolling around, but I couldn't hear him.

"Malcolm, are you playing hide and seek?"

It was quiet. Too quiet. I couldn't hear him knocking into desks or chairs.

"Malcolm…?"

I took a quick look around the room. I couldn't see his big ball. I couldn't hear him rolling around. It was like he wasn't even there…

I froze. He'd gone! He'd vanished!

If I didn't find Malcolm soon, I'd be in serious trouble. We weren't supposed to take him out of the cage without permission. Mrs Cherry would be SO angry with me. Everyone would be. I'd lost our school pet! We'd only had him for a week.

"I have to find him!" I cried. "But where could he be…?"

Chapter 5

Malcolm was missing!

I shouldn't have taken him out of the cage, I thought. We might never see him again!

I rushed around the classroom, checking under desks, chairs and behind cupboards.

"Malcolm, where are you?"

I went into the store cupboard. He wasn't there either. Just loads of paper, pens, textbooks and other stuff for class.

Suddenly I heard a bang behind me. I followed the noise to the classroom door.

It was Malcolm's ball!

"You naughty boy, I've been looking…"

I knelt down and peered inside the hamster ball. The door had been chewed off. The ball was empty.

Malcolm had gone. Gone to hide in the classroom somewhere or…he'd run into the corridor. The classroom door was open a crack because someone hadn't closed it properly. That meant Malcolm could be anywhere by now!

I knew I'd be in serious trouble. I wasn't supposed to put him in the big ball without permission. Now I'd lost the school pet. Everyone would hate me. When Mr Badal called home, my parents would be REALLY angry…

"Malcolm, where are you?" I cried.

I ran down the corridor, checking under benches and lockers. I searched in the girls' toilets. I went into the boys' toilets, just in case, but Malcolm wasn't there either.

"Malcolm!" I sobbed. "Where are you?"

Teary-eyed, I managed to see a whitish brown blur straight ahead. It shot across the floor and headed straight for the stairs.

"Malcolm!"

I wiped away my tears and dashed after him.

Malcolm was halfway downstairs, washing his face. He stood on his back legs and looked at me. I wagged my finger at him, so he looked away. He knew he'd been naughty. He knew I was going to tell him off.

"Why did you run—"

"Mya, is that you?" Mrs Cherry called from downstairs. "Is everything okay up there?"

Quickly, I ran down and grabbed Malcolm. I held him behind my back.

Mrs Cherry appeared at the bottom of the

stairs. She looked worried when she saw my face.

"Mya, what on earth is the matter?" she asked, rushing up to me. "You've been crying!"

"Um…"

As long as Malcolm got back in his cage, everything would be just fine. She didn't have to know he'd escaped, right? I'd found him. He was okay. I wouldn't be in trouble. I just needed to get him back to class.

"Miss, um, I just…" I had to think of something fast! "I just…saw a massive, hairy, ugly, mean spider!"

"Where?" She looked terrified, her eyes moving around the ceiling and walls.

"It came upstairs. If you hurry, you might catch it!"

"I can't stand spiders…I'll ask someone for help. See you back in class!"

Mrs Cherry rushed downstairs and ran away faster than Malcolm had.

Breaktime is over soon, I thought. I've got to hurry!

When Malcolm and I got back to class, I went straight over and put him in the cage. After double-checking that it was locked, I waved goodbye and went to my desk.

I could finally calm down. Or try too. My heart was still beating so fast!

I wiped my eyes with a tissue and rested my head on the desk. No one would ever know what had happened. It was Malcolm and I's little secret.

The door opened and Mrs Cherry walked in. She stopped and looked down, a puzzled look on her face.

"Mya, why is the big ball out?" she asked. "You didn't take Malcolm out without permission, did you?"

Uh oh, I thought. I'm in trouble now...

Chapter 6

"Mya, I asked you a question," Mrs Cherry said. "Why is Malcolm's ball by the door?"

"I—"

Malcolm sneezed twice.

"Bless you. Poor darling," Mrs Cherry said, rushing over to him. She poked her fingers into the cage. Malcolm placed his tiny hands on hers, which made her smile.

Then she turned back to the hamster ball. She went over and picked it up.

"Oh Mya," she said. "I can see what happened here…"

"I didn't do it on purpose, I swear!"

"I knew something fishy was going on." Mrs Cherry tutted. "That ugly spider story you told earlier sounded too strange to be true."

"Please don't be angry!"

"…Why would I be?" Mrs Cherry asked. "Malcolm chewed his ball and damaged the door lock."

"Um, yes."

"You noticed the ball was broken. You tried to fix it but ended up breaking it even more. It upset you. That's why you were crying earlier."

Just go along with it, I thought. She doesn't have to know the truth…

"Mya, some naughty hamsters try to run away. They break off the doors to escape. It happens. Next time just tell me the ball is broken, okay? I'll replace it. We don't want

Malcolm to run away."

I nodded. It was wrong to lie to people, especially adults, but I hadn't really lied. I just hadn't told her the truth. Anyway, she said I should be honest *next* time, not this time.

"I'll order a new ball this evening," she said. "Hopefully he'll feel better by tomorrow."

"Feel better?"

"He might be coming down with the cold…We'll see how he feels tomorrow."

"I'm sure he'll be just fine," I said. "My dad only has a cold for two or three days. Then he's back to normal!"

"Did you hear that, Malcolm?" Mrs Cherry said. "I'm sure you'll feel better soon."

Unfortunately, she was wrong.

Poor Malcolm wouldn't feel better tomorrow. In fact, he would feel much,

much worse…

Chapter 7

Next morning, Malcolm wasn't any better. Our happy, fit and healthy hamster had gone.

Now we had a sad, sick Malcolm who moved around like a snail. He stayed in bed all lesson and wouldn't come out to say hello at breaktime. I peeked inside his bedroom and saw him curled up, asleep.

"Is Malcolm all right?" Mrs Cherry asked. She came over and looked at his food bowl. "He hasn't eaten anything since yesterday."

I checked his water bottle.

"He hasn't drunk anything either," I said.

"And I can't see any excrement."

"Excrement?"

"Poo."

Why not just say poo, then? Fancy pants!

Don't tell her I said that...

"Maybe he sprained himself on the bars again," Mrs Cherry said. "I always worry about his widdle hands when he swings around like that. At least he's having fun...or he used to."

Fun? We both knew why he swung around like that.

He wanted to escape. Again.

One time, he stood on his back legs and pushed the bars with his hands. The bars lifted up because Angel hadn't bothered to close them properly. He slipped out. Luckily, I was there. Unluckily, he peed on my hand.

Another time, he'd swung on the bars and grabbed them with his feet too. He took a good look around to make sure no one was watching. Then he nibbled on the metal bars, but he never got out. No one can chew through metal.

"Malcolm, it's breaktime," I said. "Where are you?"

Mrs Cherry opened Malcolm's bedroom and carefully lifted the cotton wool bedding away. He barely looked at us.

I reached inside and stroked his soft fur. It was much warmer than usual. His tiny nose was cold, wet and snotty. He sneezed.

"Bless you," I said.

"Oh no. He's definitely got a cold." Mrs Cherry put her fingertip on his forehead. "He is *very* warm."

Malcolm usually hugged anyone who touched him. He didn't bother this time.

"He probably needs some rest," she said.

He half-opened his eyes and closed them.

"Let him sleep. I'll book an appointment with the vet immediately."

I wanted to kiss him goodbye, but Mrs Cherry wouldn't let me. She said it was unhygienic to kiss animals.

I stroked his scruffy head and placed some hamster chocolate by his hand. He stuffed the chocolate into his mouth and flopped back down. Mrs Cherry covered him in wool and closed his bedroom.

"You can visit him again at lunchtime." She patted my head. "Go outside for some fresh air. I don't want you catching a cold too."

"Sleep tight," I said to Malcolm. "I'll see you later."

I thought he'd sleep off his cold. Soon he'd be swinging around his cage like he used to.

I took one last look at him before leaving. I didn't realise this might be the last time I ever saw him. Our school pet was about to go missing again…

Chapter 8

Lunchtime just wasn't the same. I tried to eat but I didn't feel like it. All the food reminded me of poor Malcolm. All he ate were nuts and dried fruits. His food was so tiny and tough to nibble on.

Maybe something hot and tasty would make him feel better? Hot chocolate always made my brother Will get out of bed when he was sick. Maybe Malcolm would like a hot drink too?

"Libby, do you think Malcolm would like hot chocolate or tea?" I asked.

"I've never heard of hamsters drinking tea," she said. "Is it safe for him to eat human food?"

"I don't know, but I have to do something! He's not eating his hamster food anymore. Maybe he'd like our human food instead?"

"You mean sandwiches?" She held up her tuna and sweetcorn sandwich. "You can take one of mine."

"No thanks," I said. "I meant something really, really, REALLY tasty like...green grapes."

"You mean white grapes?"

"No. Green ones."

"Mya, the green ones are called *white* grapes."

"Nope. They're definitely *green*! I should know. I've eaten thousands."

My favourite meal in the whole world was

a bunch of fresh green grapes with a glass of cool, plain water. Other drinks messed up the taste of my sweet, juicy GREEN grapes.

I nibbled on my peanut butter sandwiches. They were so tasty. Mum always toasted them just right.

"You were right," I said to Libby. "Malcolm caught the cold. I should've listened to you before."

"It doesn't matter now," she said, patting me on the hand. "We've got to make him better."

"But how?"

"Maybe ask Mrs Cherry for help?"

"You're right! She has a cold too. She'll know what hamster medicine we can give Malcolm. Then he'll get better faster."

There was no time to lose. I could've waited until lunchtime was over, but how could I sit there eating and chatting when

Malcolm was sick? I had to do something now!

I went straight back to class and knocked on the door. I could've just walked in, but that would be rude.

"Did you hear that?" Mrs Cherry asked somebody in class. "I think someone's at the door?"

"Stop changing the subject," Mr Badal snapped. "We have to do something! Now!"

"I know that!" Mrs Cherry cried. "This can't be happening!"

"Keep your voice down," Mr Badal hissed. He could tell teachers what to do because he was the headteacher. He was in charge of the whole school.

Mrs Cherry said something very quietly, so I pressed my ear against the door.

Yes, I know I was being nosy but...

"Anyway," Mr Badal whispered, "Get rid

of it. Now!"

"Him!"

"He, she, it. Get rid. Now."

I backed away from the door as they got closer. I didn't want them to know I'd been listening.

Mr Badal threw open the door and froze when he saw me. Even though he's Asian, his skin turned as white as Mrs Cherry's. Her skin was as white as paper. "Mya, sweetie, what are you doing here?" she asked.

Mrs Cherry was holding a shopping bag with something hard inside. She put the bag behind her back and smiled, tears in her eyes.

"Mrs Cherry is not well," Mr Badal said. His light brown skin colour slowly came back. A moment later, he was Asian again. "Go back to lunch."

"Sorry, Sir, but Mrs Cherry said I could check on Malcolm."

I squeezed through them and went to Malcolm's cage. His bedroom was open and his cotton wool bedding was missing. He'd eaten all his food, including the hamster chocolate I left. I looked around but couldn't see him anywhere.

"Where's Malcolm?" I asked.

"Maybe he went for a roll," Mr Badal said with a shrug.

I looked around the room for his big ball. It wasn't there. I couldn't hear him knocking into tables and chairs.

Where is he? I wondered. If he's not in his cage or ball then…

"Where's Malcolm?" I asked Mr Badal.

"I have more important matters to deal with," Mr Badal snapped. "Mrs Cherry, sort this out."

Mr Badal rushed downstairs to his office and slammed the door shut.

Mrs Cherry closed the classroom door and waved me over to her desk. I stood beside her while she blew her nose. She tossed the tissue and took another one.

"Miss, where's Malcolm?"

"Malcolm has…gone."

"Gone where?"

"To…sleep." She wouldn't look me in the eye. "Malcolm went to sleep."

"Where is he sleeping?" I asked. "Let's wake him up!"

"We can't. He's sleeping somewhere else. I don't know where."

Mrs Cherry looked so sad. She'd been crying. Poor Miss. Her cold had blocked her nose. Crying blocked it even more.

"Mrs Cherry, what's in that bag?"

"The hamster ball door," she said, looking away.

I remembered the hamster ball was

broken. If Mrs Cherry put Malcolm in the ball, he might've chewed the door off again and ran away. That's why she was crying. She was upset because she'd lost our school pet!

"I know what really happened," I said.

"You do?" She glanced down at the plastic bag. "Who told you?"

"Nobody. I figured it out."

"Mya, this is all my fault. The others will be so upset!"

"Miss, it's not your fault," I said. "He got out of his ball and ran away before you could catch him."

She looked down at the plastic bag again and bit her bottom lip.

"...You're right, Mya. His ball was broken. I hadn't bought a new one yet. I'm sorry."

She wouldn't look in my eyes when she spoke. Some people did that when they told fibs.

"Mya, I put him in the hamster ball. He was only inside for a minute! But it was enough time for him to push off the ball's broken door and run away. He's gone!"

"It's okay," I said. "It's my job to take care of this."

"Your job? What do you mean?"

I didn't tell *everyone* I was a police officer. The Children's Police Force was a secret. We didn't want bad guys to know who we were.

"I mean my job as a *student*," I said quickly. "What other job could I have at eight years old?"

"What did you mean by taking care of this?" she asked. "Malcolm is gone. End of story. Maybe we can have another school pet someday…"

There was no way anyone was taking Malcolm's place. That was his cage, his hamster wheel, his food and his treats.

Malcolm wasn't just a school pet. He was our good friend. He was always there to listen and make someone smile.

"I will find him." I handed her a tissue from the box. "I will look around and give you a report by Friday afternoon."

"Maybe we should just let him be free?" Mrs Cherry said. "He was always trying to escape. He might be happier out there somewhere."

She looked down at the bag again.

"Miss, he's a hamster. He can't just get a job and take care of himself." I patted her hand and she smiled a little. "Let me look around. Do your job and I'll do mine."

"But—"

"Mr Badal won't be so mad when we find Malcolm."

"Thank you for helping," she said sadly. "It's my fault for not buying a new ball yesterday. I should've gone straight to the vet after school."

"Does the vet sell hamster balls?" I asked.

"No, I meant the pet shop, not the vet," she said. "There's one near my house, but I was feeling too sick and lazy to go."

She still wouldn't look me in the eye. That's something people do when they've been naughty. Or when they're keeping secrets…

Why keep secrets if you've done nothing wrong? Unless Malcolm was missing and Mrs Cherry had something to do with it. Something she wasn't telling me…

If Mrs Cherry had been bad, I would give her a chance to tell me. She'd still be in trouble, though.

"Mrs Cherry, is there anything you want to tell me?"

She gulped and shook her head, still not

looking me in the eye.

"Are you sure?" I asked.

"You should go out and play," she said, gently pushing me to the door. "Go out and keep Libby company. We don't want her playing alone, do we?"

As soon as I stepped outside, she closed the door behind me and locked it. I tried to peek inside but she pulled down the blinds.

I pressed my ear against the door. I could hear her going through the plastic bag she'd been holding. It sounded like she was crying.

Just like I'd cried when I lost Malcolm.

Maybe Mrs Cherry *was* telling the truth. She put Malcolm in the broken hamster ball and he got out again. Now he was lost in the classroom and she couldn't find him. That would explain why she was so sad.

It would also explain what Mr Badal was telling her to get rid of: Malcolm's ball. It was proof that Mrs Cherry had put Malcolm in the ball, even though she knew it was broken.

Poor Mrs Cherry. Everyone would be angry with her. She'd promised to buy a new hamster ball, but didn't. If she'd bought a new one, Malcolm couldn't have escaped.

But it was too late now.

It was time to find Malcolm. When I did, Mrs Cherry would feel much better. I wouldn't tell anyone that she'd lost him. It would be our little secret.

Malcolm couldn't have gone far, I thought. He might still be in the classroom somewhere.

At lunchtime break, I returned to class. Mrs Cherry was at her desk, blowing her red nose. She looked surprised to see me.

"Back so soon?"

"Mrs Cherry, I came to draw some MISSING posters for Malcolm. Is that okay?"

"Um yes, of course. He is missing after all…Out there somewhere having a great time with his hamster friends."

I went to his cage and looked around. There were patches of silver where he'd nibbled away the paint on the metal bars, but no hole he could crawl through. The bars were too close together for him to squeeze through.

He couldn't nibble his way out, I thought. That's why he chewed the door off his ball instead. It was his only chance to run away.

The food bowl and water bottle were empty. He'd taken enough food and water for a long trip away.

But where did he go?

Think like a hamster, I thought. I closed my eyes and imagined him rolling away in his ball. His tiny eyes were looking around, but for what? Food, maybe? Some human food? Where could he find human food? In our schoolbags!

When Mrs Cherry was busy putting out our textbooks for the next lesson, I crept over to everyone's rucksacks. They were in the cupboard at the back of class.

I shouldn't do this, I thought. Going through other people's stuff without asking is wrong...

But I did it anyway.

First I checked my bag, but Malcolm wasn't in there. Then I picked up Angel's. It was all pink and fluffy. He wasn't in there either. Just pictures of Angel with her pony, dolls and other boring photos of her having fun.

I tried Jimmy's bag next. He had a small padlock on it, so I couldn't open the zip very far. Inside was a brand-new walkie-talkie, shiny silver handcuffs, and a ham sandwich wrapped in cling film.

"Mya, what on earth are you doing?" Mrs Cherry asked. "Are you going through other people's bags without permission?"

Uh oh, I thought. I think I've been caught…

Chapter 9

"Mya, I asked why you're going through other people's bags," Mrs Cherry said, tapping her foot. "You know that is against the rules."

"I was slipping notes into their bags," I fibbed, "to tell them that Malcolm is missing."

"Oh…that's nice of you," she said, her cheeks turning bright pink. "Sorry, I thought you were being naughty. Carry on!"

Phew! I thought. I need to hurry up and finish before she realises I told a lie.

Bag after bag I searched, but Malcolm wasn't there. I stopped to think of other quiet, dark places he'd hide.

I know! I thought. He's in the cupboards!

I checked the store cupboard first. There were books, notebooks and textbooks. Malcolm wasn't there.

I went to the stationary cupboard and checked all fifty pens, pencils and a box of rubbers that were hidden at the back. There were no bite marks or pieces he'd nibbled off.

The library books were okay too. He hadn't nibbled or peed on them. There wasn't poo anywhere.

Sometimes Malcolm pooed while he was moving! He'd be eating, drinking, rolling, even sleeping, and a rock hard, tiny, brown poo would slide out.

"He might still be around," I said. "I know one way to find out!"

I hid some chocolate bits in the cupboards. I had to hide them at the back or some greedy human might take Malcolm's treats.

My plan was simple: leave some treats out. Sit through some "fun" geography class and then, when everyone else was rushing home, I'd see if any treats were missing.

"Are those treats for Malcolm?" Mrs Cherry asked.

"Yep," I replied. "They'll make him come out. Then we can catch him."

"That's a great idea," she said. "Now take your seat, please. I'll get the rest of class."

With her head down, Mrs Cherry walked out. A while later, she followed everyone back in. She went straight to her desk and turned on her computer. She kept clicking the mouse so hard I thought it'd break.

Five minutes later, everyone was still

waiting for class to start. Mrs Cherry kept clicking the mouse, her face bright pink. No one disturbed her. You shouldn't rush a teacher. If they want to waste time then let them. You get less work that way…

But I couldn't just sit there staring at the walls or clock or Jimmy, I mean Jimmy's cool, new pen that glowed in the dark. All I could think about were the treats in the cupboards.

I edged closer to the cupboards and listened out for Malcolm. I wanted to hear his sharp teeth nibbling or his tiny feet pattering about.

Instead I could hear Angel talking about herself, and Angel's friends talking about her. Jimmy and his friends talked about last night's football match. Libby was sharpening her pencils.

Mrs Cherry kept clicking and clicking the

mouse. I turned and caught her glancing at the cupboards, her nose puffy and red.

"It's been ten whole minutes since breaktime," I whispered to Libby. "What's going on? Are we gonna work or not?"

"I don't know," Libby whispered back. "There's something wrong with Mrs Cherry. She keeps looking at the cupboards and ignoring us."

I couldn't stop watching the cupboards either. I wanted to see the door open and a whisker poke out. Then there'd be a pink, runny nose and black, beady eyes. It would be Malcolm! He'd come back with a mouth full of treats.

Malcolm would stand on his back legs and spread his arms. I'd pick him up and give him the biggest hug ever.

But that was all my imagination.

When I rushed over to the cupboards and

opened the doors, the hamster chocolate was still there. Every single one.

I returned to my desk, trying not to cry.

"I'm bored," Libby said. "I'm going to do some homework."

Libby was right.

Not working is boring after a while. If Mrs Cherry was going to waste time, fine, but I wouldn't waste time too.

Waiting around for Malcolm to come back wasn't working. I had to try something else or we might never see him again.

I stood up and tapped my ruler on the desk. Everyone looked back at me.

"I'm sure you all noticed Malcolm is missing," I said.

Everyone looked shocked. I guess they hadn't noticed after all.

If they didn't know Malcolm was missing, they also didn't know Mrs Cherry had lost him. I'd promised to keep her secret, and I wouldn't break that promise…unless I *had* to.

"I'm looking for Malcolm. I'm going to find him. I need help, though."

Everyone nodded. Some girls looked like they'd cry. Even the boys looked a bit weepy.

I guess they DO care about Malcolm, I thought. Nobody seemed to care much when it was time to clean up his poo…

"Has anyone seen Malcolm running around class?" I asked.

Emma wiped her teary eyes and put her hand up.

"I saw a rat in the playground," she said sadly. "Maybe he's friends with Malcolm. I could ask him?"

"Okay, but don't get too close," I said. "I don't want it to bite you."

"A rat?" Mrs Cherry cried. "Oh dear…"

She sank into her chair and closed her eyes. She only opened them to look at the cupboards again.

"Anyone else know anything?" I asked.

Jimmy put his hand up. Hearing that Malcolm was missing made his face go pale. Except for his spots. They were still red.

"Well, I heard that some Year Six kids wanted Malcolm in their class," Jimmy said. "They said they'd take him before it was their turn. They didn't want to wait another week."

Everyone gasped.

"Why didn't you tell us before?" I asked.

"I hear lots of things," he said. "Lots of things that never happen. I thought they were fibbing. I guess they weren't."

I couldn't believe it. Had the Year Six kids stolen Malcolm? Every class was going to have a turn caring for him. Why couldn't the older kids just wait like everybody else?

"Class," Mrs Cherry said, "I am sure Year Six did not kidnap Malcolm. He is out there somewhere running around. Happy and healthy as can be."

I didn't believe her. She was covering for Year Six so there wouldn't be trouble in the playground.

"Class, I'm sure Year Six had nothing to do with Malcolm's disappearance."

Well, I was sure they DID have something to do with him going missing. I just needed to find some proof. It wouldn't be easy. The Year Six kids were older than us. Bigger than us. Smarter than us.

But they weren't better than us.

Year Six won't get away with this, I thought. I'm going to their classroom and bringing Malcolm back!

I thought it'd be easy. I'd go to Year Six,

tell them off and get Malcolm back. But I didn't realise how mean Year Six could be.

I was about to find out.

They didn't like younger kids in their classroom. The last person caught snooping around in there was never seen again…

Chapter 10

"Are you really going to Year Six?" Jimmy asked. His eyes widened and his white skin turned very pale. "Year Six students can be so mean. You can't go there by yourself."

"You coming with me?" I asked.

"I, um, no…" He glanced over at his friends. "We've got a football match at breaktime. I can't let the team down."

"You're not coming because you're scared," I said. "It's okay. Everyone's scared sometimes."

"I am NOT scared," he snapped. "I'm

just...very busy with footie."

I looked around the classroom. No one looked me in the eye. Nobody offered to help. Even Angel looked scared. She was the meanest girl at school, but she didn't mess with Year Six either.

"What's everyone so scared of?" I asked. "They're just like us but bigger, that's all."

We were Year Four. That meant everyone in Nursery, Reception class, Year One, Year Two and Year Three looked up to us.

But *everyone* looked up to Year Six.

Everybody was jealous of Year Six. They got the best school trips and the biggest school prizes. In a few months, they'd get to leave primary school and go to secondary school.

I didn't know what secondary school was like, but I did know Mr Badal wouldn't be there. That's why I couldn't wait to leave. I would miss my friends though…

But not even my friends were being helpful today. They were all too scared to come with me to Year Six.

"Don't go," Libby whispered. "Please don't…"

I felt bad about leaving her. If Year Six locked me in their classroom, I might never escape! Would she get a new best friend? It would be hard because she was very, very shy.

I've got to come back, I thought. I won't leave Libby alone!

Everyone looked at the clock on the wall. In five minutes, the bell would ring. Breaktime would start. Then I'd be off to Year Six.

I was going to get our hamster back!

"I bet she won't do it," Angel said. "She'll chicken out."

"Please don't go," Libby whispered to me.

"What if something bad happens?"

"Like what?" I asked, my heart beating a little faster.

"Ask Emma."

"Ask Emma what?" I asked. "Emma, what do you know about Year Six?"

Everyone leaned in closer to Emma. She checked over her shoulder like someone might be watching. The only other person there was Mrs Cherry, but she was busy cleaning the whiteboard.

"Do you really wanna know?" Emma asked, her brown skin going pale. She was sweating so hard that her curly hair was stringy and wet. "I don't like talking about this…"

"I'm sure it's not *that* bad," I said, shaking a little. "Go on!"

"Boys and girls," Emma began, "a very long time ago (maybe last year) a boy said he was going to Year Six. He said Year Six took his football at breaktime and wouldn't give it back."

"Why didn't he tell the teachers?" I asked.

"Because everyone knows they like Year Six the best," she said. "That's why Year Six gets a holiday at the end of the year. All we get is homework."

Everyone nodded. It just wasn't fair that the older kids got all the best stuff.

"Anyway," Emma continued, "the boy was in Year Five. He thought he was big enough to stand up to Year Six. Well, he was wrong…"

"What happened?" I asked, starting to sweat.

"Nobody really knows. We've got a new Year Six now. The old Year Six kept the truth a secret. Now they're at secondary school, so we can't ask them what happened…"

"So how'd you know something bad happened?" I asked, shaking a little. "I mean did he leave a letter or something?"

"The only thing he left behind was a lunchbox with a mouldy apple inside."

Someone gasped. A girl started crying.

"So they never saw him again?" I asked.

"My big sister said the lunchbox is still in the Year Six classroom. Nobody touches it. They left it there so everyone knows how strong Year Six is."

Jimmy asked, "What happened to the apple?"

"My sister said it's still there. It'll stay there forever and ever." Emma turned to me. "You'll stay there too if they catch you. I heard there's lots of younger kids locked in the Year Six store cupboard."

"Can't they just walk out?" I asked.

"Not if the *teacher* locks them in!"

We all gasped.

"Is the Year Six teacher mean too?" I asked.

Emma nodded. "I heard he's meaner and scarier than Mr Badal."

A teacher has to be REALLY scary if they're scarier than the headteacher.

"Don't let the Year Six teacher catch you," Emma said. "Don't let Year Six catch you either…"

"Class, get ready for breaktime," Mrs Cherry said. "Everyone must go out today. I'll be locking the classroom."

Everyone turned to the clock.

Tick tock. Tick tock. Tick tock.

Thirty seconds to go…

Twenty seconds to go…

Ten seconds to go…

Five…four…three…two…one.

The bell rang.

I've got to be brave, I thought. I'm a police officer. A good police officer must be brave.

I marched to the door and threw it open. I looked back at everyone. They all looked as scared as I felt.

"I'll see you guys in fifteen minutes," I said. "Don't be late."

I walked down the corridor, my eyes on the Year Six door straight ahead. I held my head high. I didn't want them thinking I was scared.

But I *was* scared. Very scared.

Were there kids locked in the Year Six store cupboard? I thought they just had paper, books and pens in there. I didn't know you could lock people in store cupboards too. It was such a mean thing to do.

Would they lock me in there too? I might stay in there forever and ever. I'd never see my family again. I'd never see my friends again. I'd never see Malcolm again.

I can't let that happen, I thought to myself. I've got to be brave!

Whenever I was scared, my mum said this: "Everything you want is on the other side of fear." It was her favourite quote.

"Mya," she'd say, "think about what you want, not what you're afraid of. Be positive, not negative."

That's why I had to stay positive. I had to think of what I wanted.

I wanted Malcolm back.

I can do this, I thought. I will do this.

When I reached the Year Six door, I grabbed the handle and held on tight. I looked back and my class was watching from far behind. I couldn't go back now. They were counting on me.

Come on Mya, I thought. You can do this!

After a few very deep breaths, I opened the

door and stepped inside...

Chapter 11

Nobody was there. Year Six had all gone out to play. Their mean teacher wasn't there either. Good. I didn't want to meet anyone meaner than Mr Badal.

This was the first time I'd ever been in the Year Six classroom. I heard it was bigger and better than all the other classrooms.

That wasn't true.

The Year Six classroom was the same size as everyone else's, but it felt smaller because it was packed with stuff. There were thick textbooks on every shelf, educational posters all over the walls, and the desks couldn't close properly because there was so much inside. On the whiteboard were two calendars packed with things to do. It looked like they never got a break.

I crept over to the teacher's desk and looked over his things. There were piles of worksheets that looked like exams and homework. I wasn't looking forward to doing all that work one day...

In Year Four, our weekly homework was a book to read or twenty questions to answer. Sometimes we had scrapbook work, but that was fun. Year Six's homework didn't look fun at all.

You didn't come here to be nosy, I thought. Find Malcolm!

I didn't see anything about Malcolm on the teacher's desk, so I opened his drawers. It was a naughty thing to do but...

"Hamster food!"

Inside the drawer was a small pack of hamster food. There were nuts, oats and dried fruit. It looked just like the food Malcolm ate.

"They bought hamster food so they can keep him here," I said. "What else did they buy for him?"

I rushed over to the store cupboard. I pressed my ear against the door and listened closely.

Silence. It didn't sound like anybody was locked in there. Just in case, I knocked three times and waited.

"Maybe Emma was wrong," I said. "Maybe nobody's in there…"

I turned the door knob slowly and pulled the door open. I peeked inside, but it was too dark to see anything.

My heart racing, I opened the door wider

and stepped inside. There was a light switch beside me. I pressed it.

There was no one else in there. I was happy about that. But I wasn't happy about the big bag of cotton wool in the corner. It looked like the wool Malcolm slept on.

"They've got his food and his bedding," I said, "but where is he?"

Something tapped the window. I shrugged it off. Then it happened again.

I tiptoed over and peered outside. Down in the playground, Jimmy and Libby were waving madly at me. Jimmy had a pile of tiny stones at his feet. He must've been throwing them at the window to get my attention.

I opened the window.

"What is it?" I asked. "I can't talk now!"

"Get out," Jimmy yelled. "I heard some Year Six boys talking. They're going back to class for something. You've gotta hide!"

Heavy footsteps stomped upstairs. I ran to the cupboard and closed it. I could've hidden in there, but what if they locked me in? I didn't want to be like that boy who went missing last year.

I ran to the teacher's desk and hid underneath. As long as they didn't come over there, no one would see me.

Maybe they've forgotten their coats or something, I thought. Or maybe they want their crisps or drinks or…Malcolm? Maybe they're coming to get Malcolm!

I peeked under the desk so I could watch them. If they were coming for Malcolm, I needed to know where he was.

The classroom door flew open and five Year Six boys walked in. Two of them started playfighting on the carpet. Two of them talked about Christmas presents.

The fifth boy stopped in the middle of the

room. He didn't say anything, he just stood there looking around.

"What's wrong, Jamar?" one of the boys asked.

Jamar, the fifth boy, kept looking around the room. His big, brown eyes stopped on the window I'd opened. He scratched his curly, brown hair, looking confused.

"That window was locked when we left class," Jamar said. "Who opened it?"

"Who cares?" one boy said. "Anyway, I want a new bike for Christmas, but my mum said no…"

Jamar walked to the cupboard and opened the door. That's when I realised the light was still on!

"Who left the light on?" Jamar asked. His light brown skin went very pale. He looked worried, but his friends didn't seem to notice.

"Is someone in here?" Jamar asked.

"Hello? Anybody there?"

I kept perfectly still. I breathed as quietly as possible.

Slowly Jamar went from cupboard to cupboard. He opened the doors, looked inside and then moved on.

"Jamar, just get your coat! Breaktime is over in ten!"

"No," Jamar snapped. "Someone is in here. I can feel it."

"They couldn't fit in the cupboards unless they're really small," the Christmas bike boy said. "Do you think...?"

The other boys stopped playfighting and stood by Jamar. They looked very angry now.

"One of the younger kids in *our* classroom?" one boy said, his white face turning red. "Why? It's OUR classroom, not theirs!"

The others nodded.

"Look, just calm down, all right?" Jamar said. "It might be some Nursery kid."

"Then we'd better find them before they get stuck somewhere."

Three of the boys started looking through each cupboard. Two went to the store cupboard and looked around in there.

If I tiptoe quietly and quickly, I thought, I might get to the door!

Everyone's back was turned to me. If I ran quickly and slipped out the door, they wouldn't know I was there.

What about Malcolm? I thought. I can't just leave him here!

"Jamar," one of the boys said, "there's nobody here!"

"I guess you're right." Jamar shrugged. "I just feel like someone's watching me."

"Can we go now?"

Jamar nodded.

The other boys left the classroom. Jamar was the last to go. He quickly looked around one more time before walking out.

I sighed with relief. Part of me was happy they'd gone. I was lucky I hadn't been caught.

But the other part of me was sad. They'd looked through every cupboard and Malcolm hadn't been there.

"Maybe they hid him somewhere else," I said. "I should follow those boys. They'll lead me straight to Malcolm!"

Before leaving, I went to the window and waved at Libby and Jimmy. They both looked happy to see me. I also saw Jamar's friends walking outside but I didn't see him there.

I have to get out of here, I thought. Their teacher might be back soon!

I ran to the door and pressed my ear

against it. The stairs were so close, but I couldn't leave yet. Nearby, Mrs Cherry was chatting to Mrs Tipple, Year Five's teacher. Mrs Tipple was the same height as me and looked so young.

"Madison," Mrs Tipple cried, "you have to tell them the truth!"

"I can't do it," Mrs Cherry said. "They're still quite young. I'm not sure they'll understand."

"That's life. It happens. One day it'll happen to all of us."

"It's easier for you," Mrs Cherry said. "Your students are older. Mine are only eight or nine."

"Just tell them Malcolm—"

"Quiet," Mrs Cherry snapped. "Someone might hear us. Let's talk in my room."

Seconds later, a door closed. Now the corridor was silent.

"Get going," I said. "I've got to follow Jamar and his friends! They'll lead me straight to Malcolm."

I opened the door and gasped.

Standing right there was Jamar. He didn't look angry or sad or anything. He just stared at me.

"Why are you following me and my friends?" he asked, stepping closer to me.

I gulped, stepping back. I couldn't tell him about Malcolm. Year Six would know I was looking for him.

"I'm…new," I said. "I heard that you're in Year Six. Year Six students help people, right?"

"Yeah, I'm in Year Six. So what?"

"I just wanted to say hello, that's all."

I tried to step past him but he wouldn't let me. I stepped to the left, he stepped to the left. I stepped to the right, he stepped to the right.

"Who are you?" he asked. He towered over me. I'd never seen a student so tall!

"I'm…Maggie?"

"You're fibbing," he said. "What year are you in?"

"Year…Five?"

"You're too small for Year Five," he said. "I'd say you're in Year Three or Year Four."

He stepped closer to me, so I stepped back. He closed the door behind him, looking down his nose at me.

"You're snooping around our class. Why? Why did you look in our store cupboard?"

"Was someone in there?" I asked, playing dumb.

"The light was on!"

"Maybe someone else left it on," I said. "How'd you know *I* left it on?"

"None of your business how I know," he

snapped. "Trust me. I see everything around here. Now tell me what you're doing in our classroom!"

"I told you already. I just came to say hello!"

"You told me that lie before," he said. "Now tell me the truth."

I couldn't tell him the truth. How could I trust him? He might be the one who stole our hamster!

"Okay, fine," he said. "You don't have to say anything to me."

He pulled over a chair and sat right in front of the door.

"What're you doing?" I asked.

"Maggie, or whatever your real name is, we're going to sit here until my teacher comes back. You can tell him who you really are. You can tell him why you were snooping around his desk earlier."

How did he know that? He wasn't even there at the time!

"So, Maggie, what's it gonna be? Are you going to tell me the truth?" He leaned in. "Or will you talk to my teacher?"

I couldn't talk to a mean Year Six boy like him, but I couldn't talk to a mean Year Six teacher either. Jamar might pick on me but his teacher could give me days or weeks in detention.

"What's it gonna be, *Maggie*?" Jamar said. "Will you talk to me or my teacher? You've got ten seconds to decide…"

Chapter 12

"I won't ask you again," Jamar said, leaning forward in his chair. "Why did you snoop around our classroom?"

Time was ticking. Year Six would be back in five minutes. I could hear all the teachers heading downstairs.

"I can't tell you," I said. "It's a secret."

"A secret, eh?" He leaned in closer until our noses were touching. "If you keep this secret, you'll be in serious trouble. Are you okay with that?"

"Yep…Maybe…I guess."

Serious trouble? Me? I didn't *ever* get into trouble. I was always good because it was the right thing to do. Good police officers do the right thing, not the wrong thing.

"Fine, then." Jamar shrugged. "You'll get into trouble. You can be a bad girl if you like, but you won't get away with it."

A bad girl? Me? I didn't like him calling me that. I was a good girl. A *very* good girl. That's why I was looking for Malcolm. No one else was.

If I was already in trouble then I had nothing to be scared of anymore. I could say anything I liked to him and there was nothing more he could do about it.

I pushed my head against his. Now our noses were both very squashed. For a moment, he looked very surprised. Then he pushed back with his nose, squashing mine even more.

"I'm NOT scared of you," I said. "Now *I'm* gonna ask the questions!"

"Go ahead," he said. "You're not scared of me, I'm not scared of you."

"Where is he?"

"Who?"

"Don't answer questions with a question," I said. "My mum hates that."

"No, I mean who're you talking about?" he asked. "You asked where "he" is? Who is *he*? Does he have a name or something?"

"Malcolm!"

"Malcolm Jones in Year Three? Malcolm Peterson in Year Five? Or Malcolm Badal in Year One?"

"Malcolm the hamster!" I cried. "He's not in our classroom. Where is he?"

"I don't know. Maybe another class has him," Jamar said. "Malcolm belongs to the *whole* school, remember? You can't keep him all to yourself."

"I know that," I snapped, "but we were supposed to have him for two whole weeks! Where is he? We want him back!"

Jamar's face changed from very angry to very confused.

"You don't know where Malcolm is?" he asked. "You mean he's missing? I wasn't told about this…"

"Why would you be?"

"Because Malcolm is the *school* pet. He belongs to everyone, not just your class. We all care about him, not just you."

"If you really cared about Malcolm, you wouldn't have stolen him from us."

"Stolen him? We didn't steal him!"

"Yes, you did!"

"Really? You got proof of that?"

I rushed over to the teacher's desk and pulled out the bag of hamster food.

"You bought this hamster food so Malcolm could live here with Year Six!"

"Hamster food?" Jamar burst out laughing. "This isn't hamster food, silly. This is granola. Granola is nuts and seeds. Granola is human food, not hamster food."

I wasn't sure if he was telling the truth or not. The granola looked just like hamster food to me.

Jamar tore a tiny hole in the bag and shook out some granola. He popped it into his mouth and chewed.

"It's delicious," he said, taking my hand. Before I could say no, he poured a little granola onto my palm. "Go on. Try it."

I nibbled on it. It wasn't delicious, but it tasted pretty good. I finished the rest in my hand and took a bit more.

"That's enough," he said. "Mr Hardy will know it's been opened if we eat any more."

Jamar returned the bag to Mr Hardy's desk.

"What about the hamster bedding?" I asked, pointing at the store cupboard.

"Our store cupboard is *huge* because we've got so much work to do. That's why we keep Malcolm's things in there. I bet your store cupboard isn't big enough for all his hamster stuff."

Jamar and I sat down by the window. People were putting toys away outside. The teachers were lining up. Everyone would come in soon.

"Let's start again, okay?" Jamar said. "I'm Jamar. What's your real name?"

"I'm…I'm Mya."

"Mya…?" His eyes widened. "Mya Dove, right?"

"How'd you know?"

Jamar stood up and stomped his foot three

times.

The Children's Police Force had a secret code. It started with one officer stomping their foot three times. Was Jamar in the Children's Police Force? There was only one way to find out…

Chapter 13

Jamar stomped his foot three times

I stomped my foot twice.

He stomped once.

"What's the password?" he asked.

"Children's Police Force," I replied.

"I am Chief Superintendent Jamar Roberts."

"I am Detective Inspector Mya Dove."

My police officer name was Detective Inspector Mya Dove. I got my top secret cases from the Superintendent. We met in the girls' toilets. She never showed her face to me. I didn't know her name either. That's why I called her my secret boss.

My secret boss told me the Chief Superintendent's name was also a secret. We didn't want bad guys to know who he was. If they found out his name, they might do something mean to him like hide his homework. That's why I felt so special. Jamar trusted me with his secret identity.

"Mya, are you okay?" he asked.

"Yes, Sir!"

Jamar offered his hand. I shook it.

I couldn't believe it! I was shaking hands with the Chief Superintendent! He was the top police officer at school. He was bigger and better than my secret boss!

The Chief Superintendent could tell every officer what to do. He was in charge of the Children's Police Force, just like Mr Badal was in charge of our school.

Meeting Jamar was a dream come true. I wanted to be just like him someday. Only the best police officers could be the Chief Superintendent.

Chief Superintendent, Superintendent, Detective Inspector...you might be a bit confused right now. Here's an easy way to understand everything:

Chief Superintendent = Headteacher

The Chief Superintendent is in charge of Superintendents, just like the Headteacher is in charge of Teachers.

Superintendent = Teacher

The Superintendent is in charge of Inspectors, just like Teachers are in charge of Students.

Inspector = Student

The Inspector is in charge of cases, just like Students are in charge of homework.

Chief Superintendent = Headteacher
Superintendent = Teacher
Inspector = Student

If I worked very hard, next year I could be the Superintendent. Then in Year Six, I'd be the Chief Superintendent.

But that was two years away...

"You can stop staring now," Jamar said.

I let go of his hand. I wasn't sure how long I'd been staring at him with my mouth wide open. It was embarrassing!

"Detective, are you telling me that Malcolm is missing?"

I nodded.

"I need you to find him."

"Why can't *you* do it?" I asked. "You're the best police officer at school. You could find him much faster than me."

"I'm too busy."

Too busy? I couldn't believe what he was saying! How could he be too busy to do his job? Sure, we had lots of schoolwork but we had TWO jobs to do. Be a student and be a police officer!

"Um, Mr Chief Superintendent?"

"Break's almost over. We'd better be quick."

"Could you tell me why you're too busy to find Malcolm?"

Jamar pointed at the posters on the walls, the writing on the whiteboard, and the stacks of books on the windowsill.

"I'm too busy," he said. "Look at all the

work we've got to do."

I rolled my eyes.

"Why'd you do that?" he asked, looking a little hurt. "I'm telling the truth!"

"You Year Six are so mean," I snapped. "You think just because you're bigger and smarter that you're better than everyone else, but you're not!"

"It's not like that. I'm not trying to be mean, I swear!"

"I wish I hadn't come here," I said. "I finally get to meet the best police officer in school and he doesn't even care about my case…"

I looked away and fought back tears. I didn't want him to see me cry.

Jamar slowly turned my head and looked me right in the eye.

"I'm sorry," he said.

"You're…sorry?"

"I was mean. I didn't want to help you. I'm sorry."

He looked so sad! I couldn't be angry anymore.

"Okay, I forgive you."

"And I'm sorry if any older kids are mean to you. It's just so hard being in Year Six."

"Hard? But you get so much cool stuff! You have the biggest store cupboard. You get more books to read. You even get the best school trip. No other class gets to leave home for a whole week!"

"Do you know why we have the biggest store cupboard?"

"Because the teachers like you best!"

"Because in Year Six we have more work than any other class. That's why we have more books. We don't get more fun books to read. We get more textbooks to study."

"So you're smarter because you have more

work?" I asked.

"Yep. You'll be just as smart someday."

"What about the school trip? And you get a school dance too!"

"That's true, but only because we have to work so hard all year," he said. "We're mean sometimes because we feel a bit jealous. We get so much classwork while younger kids have all the fun..."

Jamar looked sad again. I didn't know what to do, so I patted him on the hand.

"You should be happy," I said. "Next year you'll be in Year Seven! At a different school. You'll never have to see Mr Badal again."

"But I don't want to go," he said. "I don't want to be in Year Seven."

I wanted to go to secondary school like my brother Will. His school was HUGE. They had a library, bigger gym, nicer school meals and got to go anywhere they liked at breaktime.

"Jamar, you'll love secondary school. My brother said it's amazing!"

"My sister said the same thing, but…I'm still *scared*."

"Why?" I asked.

"In Year Six, we're the biggest kids at primary school. In Year Seven, we're the smallest kids at secondary school. I don't want to be small again…"

"Why not? What's wrong with being small? Great things start small. You are proof of that."

"I am? How?"

"You started small in Nursery, right? It was just you and a tiny badge you made yourself. But you worked really hard and became Chief Superintendent Jamar Roberts. That's a great thing!"

"I went from a small police officer to a

great Chief Superintendent," he said, smiling. "All because great things start small."

"Exactly," I said. "You started small and became great at primary school. Who says you can't do it again at secondary school?"

Jamar nodded. He didn't look sad anymore. He looked very proud of himself.

"You're right," he said. "I'll start small and do great things at secondary school, college, university and one day...at a *real* police station. I'm going to be the best Chief Superintendent ever!"

The bell rang.

I turned to leave but he grabbed my hand and gently pulled me back.

"Let's find Malcolm together," he said. "Meet me at lunchtime. We'll talk more then, okay?"

I waved goodbye and rushed to the toilets. When my class walked by, I slipped out and followed everyone into the classroom.

"Everyone, continue from chapter three," Mrs Cherry said, her nose bright pink and her eyes puffy. It looked like she'd been crying.

We took out our textbooks and everyone asked me about Year Six.

"What's their classroom like?" Mark asked. "I heard it's five times bigger than ours!"

"I heard Year Six gets to eat sweets and chocolates in class," Patrice said. "Did you bring any back for us?"

"Did they try to lock you in the store cupboard?" Emma asked. "You're lucky if they didn't!"

"Did you get caught?" Jimmy asked. "I saw a boy up there. Did he see you?"

I wanted to answer everyone's questions, but I had to do something very important first.

"What's wrong?" Jimmy asked.

"I've got to check the cupboards."

"Why?"

"Because I left food for Malcolm. If the food is gone it means he's still in class somewhere."

"What if the food is still there?"

"That means he's not in class," I said. "He could be somewhere else in school or…"

I didn't want to say it, so Jimmy did.

"Or he left school."

It would be hard to find Malcolm somewhere in school. It would be *impossible* to find him outside of school.

I was starting to wonder if we'd ever see him again…

"Let's stay positive," I said. "I'm sure he's still around here somewhere. He's probably watching us right now!"

"I hope you're right."

"Of course I am," I said. "I'll check the cupboards for any clues. They'll lead right to Malcolm's secret hiding place."

There *was* a clue in the cupboard, but it wouldn't lead to a hiding place. Instead, it led to a brand-new suspect, someone nobody was expecting…

Chapter 14

I'd left food for Malcolm in our classroom cupboards. If the food was missing, it'd prove he was hiding in class somewhere. Now I had to check the cupboards, but I was too nervous to do it.

Be brave, I told myself. You can do this!

I put my hand up.

"Yes, Mya?" Mrs Cherry said.

"Miss, I left food for Malcolm in the cupboards. Can I see if he ate them?"

Mrs Cherry bit her lip and looked to the side. Her furry eyebrows were twitching.

"If you *must* look, go ahead."

I sprung up and rushed over to the cupboards. I opened the first cupboard. All the hamster food was right where I'd left it.

It's okay, I told myself. Maybe he got food from the other cupboards.

But the second cupboard was the same. The food hadn't been touched.

One more cupboard, I told myself. I hope he's been in here!

I opened the doors and looked around…

The food had gone! Malcolm must've eaten it and left.

"He's been in here!" I cried. "The food's gone!"

"Great news!" Mrs Cherry said, sighing with relief. "I'm sure he packed lots of food before leaving. At least we know he'll be well-fed on his journey."

"Journey?" I asked.

"People pack food before going on long trips," Mrs Cherry said. "Unfortunately, taking all that food means he won't return for a very long time…if ever."

"But—"

"Class, we will be ordering some new story books! I'll pass around the book catalogue with a sheet of paper."

"But Miss," I cried, "Malcolm needs us to take care of him. That's what you said!"

Mrs Cherry wiped her sweaty forehead before continuing. She didn't even look my way.

"Please write down the books you want," she said to the class. "The five most popular books will be ordered."

"Miss—"

"Mya Dove, please return to your seat. We have a lot of work to do." She placed the book catalogue and paper down on Angel's desk.

"Write quickly and pass it around. Everyone, get your pens ready. You'll be taking notes for the rest of class."

I tried not to, but I started crying. I couldn't help it. I turned away before Angel and her mean friends saw me. They would've laughed.

When I turned back to the cupboard, I spotted something at the bottom. I picked it up and was shocked by what I saw!

It was a dark, red hair. Just like the ones on Mrs Cherry's head. The hair hadn't been there before I left. That meant she'd been in the cupboard at breaktime.

She's a teacher, I thought. They look inside cupboards like everyone else.

True, but she was acting very strangely. She'd been sneaking around with Mr Badal the day Malcolm went missing. And she'd been talking about something secret to Mrs

Tipple at breaktime.

I needed to think about this, but I couldn't do it here. I went back to my desk.

I was the last person to choose stories from the book catalogue. It was hard to read the words because there were still tears in my eyes.

Mrs Cherry came over to collect the catalogue and paper we'd written on. She was smiling until she saw my teary eyes.

"Answer all the questions on the board," she said sternly to everyone else. Then she knelt down beside me.

"Mya, what's wrong?"

"Miss, why was your hair in the cupboard?" I asked. "It was where I'd left Malcolm's food."

She gulped, her eyes moving from me to Libby.

"Mya, help Libby with her work. You're

very good at answering questions."

"What about Malcolm?" I asked.

"He must be long gone by now. I'm sure that wherever he is, he is very happy."

"But he's *missing*! Should we call the police?"

"No need for all that," she said. "I'm sure he had good reasons to leave. Maybe he went back to his hamster family." She smiled, but her eyes looked sad.

Mrs Cherry was not being very helpful. Actually, she was being very *unhelpful*! It was like she wanted me to forget all about Malcolm. I couldn't do that! Malcolm was my friend.

Then I wondered…What if Malcolm hadn't taken the food from the cupboard? What if Mrs Cherry had taken it instead? That's why her hair was left in there. It'd fallen there by accident.

But why did she want us to think Malcolm had eaten the food? Why was she being so sneaky? Teachers are usually good, not naughty.

That's when I realised what was really going on.

Year Six didn't steal Malcolm.

Mrs Cherry did…

Chapter 15

Jamar was waiting outside the lunch hall. It was always so noisy in there. Lots of talking and lots of eating. It was much quieter in the corridor.

"How'd it go?" he asked. "Did Malcolm eat the food?"

I shook my head.

I told him Mrs Cherry took the hamster food in the cupboard. I also told him she'd been talking to Mr Badal about something yesterday.

"You really think she stole Malcolm?" he

asked. "Why would she? She could just get her own hamster, you know?"

"Malcolm is the best hamster in the world," I said. "There'll never be another hamster like him. Never!"

Jamar started pacing up and down the corridor. He rubbed his chin like my dad did when he thought about something.

"What's the plan?" I asked.

"A big secret never stays secret for long. If the teachers are up to something, someone has to be gossiping about it."

"How can we get them to talk?" I asked. "Members of staff never tell students the juiciest school gossip."

"But I'm not just any student…"

Jamar reached into his trouser pocket and pulled out a small, round badge. It was shiny and dark blue with the word PREFECT on it.

"You're a…Prefect?"

Prefects were the *best* students at school. They never had days off unless they were sick. They never came late, even on snow days. They never got told off either.

Prefects were perfect.

"So you're a Prefect AND Chief Superintendent?" I rubbed my eyes, wondering if this was really happening. "You're…AMAZING!"

"Nah, I'm just me."

He pinned the badge to his jumper and stood up straight. Now he looked even taller than before.

"When I need the latest gossip," he said, "I go straight to the person with the biggest mouth in school."

"Who's that?"

"Follow me." He took my hand and led me into the lunch hall.

First people were staring because we were holding hands. Nobody in Year Six ever held hands with the younger kids.

Then people were staring at Jamar's Prefect badge. I wanted to stare at it too. It was so shiny!

Jamar led me straight to the dinner ladies. They were gossiping by the water fountain. They barely looked at me before turning to Jamar.

"Good afternoon, ladies," Jamar said. "You all look lovely, as usual."

They batted their eyelids.

"The lunch today was delicious," Jamar said. "The tuna and sweetcorn sandwiches were so juicy and fresh. The bread was so bouncy and soft. I had to stop myself from eating *all* the sandwiches!"

"Stop it, you silly boy," Mrs Gable, the oldest dinner lady, said. "You're making me blush!"

"Mrs Gable, could I talk to you for a moment?"

The other dinner ladies went into the kitchen and closed the door behind them.

Mrs Gable waved us over to the side where it was a bit quieter. Now we could talk without being disturbed.

Mrs Gable was a redhead like Mrs Cherry, but Gable's hair was light red and curly. Her frizzy curls were covered by a very tight hairnet that pulled her eyes back, making her always look really shocked.

She was *very* chubby because she tasted all the food before serving it, just like my mum did. Mum always tasted a teaspoonful of her own cooking. Mrs Gable tasted more than that. She took a big bowl of each lunch meal and a small bowl of each dessert.

At least Mrs Gable enjoyed her cooking.

No one else did. Her food tasted like toilet paper.

Not that I've ever chewed toilet paper...

"No grapes this week," Mrs Gable said to me, her voice gruff like a man. "Mr Badal said they're too expensive."

"But they're worth it!" I cried. "What about next week?"

"Don't count on it, kid." She patted my head. Her hand smelt of burnt food. "Better learn to like apples and bananas instead."

I sighed, shaking my head.

"Anyway, how can I help my favourite student?" she asked Jamar. "No one appreciates my cooking like you do. Not even my husband and kids."

"Not everyone has good taste like us," Jamar said quietly. "Oh well! If they don't want it, that's fine with me. More food for us to eat!"

"Ain't that right!" She cackled like witches do in the movies. "Anyway, how can I help the sweetest boy at school?"

"Mrs Gable, you know I'm a Prefect?"

She nodded.

"Well, I take my job very seriously. I care about the school. I care about everyone...including the teachers."

"Go on," she said, edging closer.

"Well, I'm worried about Mrs Cherry. The teacher of Year Four."

"She looked very upset about...you know. The school pet thing." Mrs Gable shook her head sadly. "Has she told her class yet?"

"Told them what?" Jamar asked.

"I shouldn't be telling you this but someone has to." Mrs Gable wouldn't look Jamar or me in the eye. "Well, sorry to say but on Wednesday the school pet..."

Chapter 16

Mrs Gable opened her mouth to speak but nothing came out. Then her eyes slowly moved to me.

"What happened to our hamster?" I asked. "Have you seen him around?"

"Not in *my* kitchen!" she spat. "That would be unhygienic."

"Malcolm licked himself clean every day," I said. "He was very hygienic!"

"I'm surprised she knew what hygienic meant," Mrs Gable mumbled.

I was surprised too, but I didn't tell her

that.

I peeked over the food counter and looked around the kitchen. I called for Malcolm, but he didn't come out. But I did see something very interesting…

Near the door was a mousetrap. It had a little door that closed if a mouse went inside. Then people could pick up the trap and take it far, far away. The mouse would be let out so it could live somewhere else.

"Why do you have mousetraps in there?" I asked.

"No comment," Mrs Gable snapped.

"My friend saw rat traps in the playground. Maybe you have rats in the kitchen too?"

She turned really pale. Her curly fringe stuck to her sweaty forehead.

"We don't have rats," she snapped.

I peered over the counter and saw a

mousetrap by the fridge door.

"Better safe than sorry," she said. "Prevention is better than cure. You know the rest."

"Does Mr Badal know about the traps?" I gently pulled her closer. "What if Malcolm gets caught in a trap?"

"Who?"

"Our hamster. The one in Mrs Cherry's class."

"I heard that thing—"

"Is missing. We know! Has he been in the kitchen?"

"I'd know if he had been," she said, looking like she'd seen a ghost. "So, after what happened, he's still around here? Terrible, that is! Just put him outside somewhere. That's what I did with my dog when he…crossed over."

"Crossed over the road?" I asked.

"No, I mean he passed on."

"Passed on what? Human food?" I tutted. "Mrs Gable, you shouldn't give pets people food. It's wrong."

"No, I mean my dog…you know. Your hamster…you know."

"Mrs Gable!" Jamar gasped. "Are you saying that Malcolm is…?"

Jamar turned pale. His eyes moved away from mine. I tugged on his sleeve but he wouldn't say anything.

"Talk to your little friend," Mrs Gable whispered to him. "I know it's hard telling kids these things but…someone's gotta do it."

Mrs Gable patted me on the head and rushed back into the kitchen. She pulled down the shutter so we couldn't see over the counter anymore.

Jamar looked very, very sad. He went to

the window and stared outside. I stood by him, not knowing what to say.

"Are you okay?" I asked.

"I think Mrs Gable said that Malcolm is…gone?"

"But we knew that already!"

"No, I mean he's…" Jamar shook his head. "It can't be. She must be confused. It wouldn't be the first time she heard gossip wrong."

"What do you mean?"

"Last year she said Mr Badal was moving to Australia. We were so excited about having a new headteacher."

"But he's still here…"

"Unfortunately, yeah. It turns out he only went on holiday. I was so sad when he showed up."

"Mrs Gable might be wrong again," I said. "Maybe Malcolm never "passed on" like she said, whatever that means."

"Exactly. Malcolm can't be…That's just what the hamster thief wants us to think."

"So what do we—"

Someone gently poked me in the arm, so I looked back. It was Libby. She was still very shy around other people, so I led her away from Jamar.

Libby and I went out into the corridor. She had a quiet voice. It was easier to hear her when no one else was around.

"Libby, what's wrong?"

"You said that one day I could help with your cases."

"Have you found something out?"

"I remembered something strange I saw on Wednesday. It was in Mr Badal's office when I did my speech practise."

Mr Badal was the meanest headteacher in the world, but he was always nice to Libby.

She was really shy, so he helped her practise speaking. It'd only been a week or two but she was already doing better.

"What did you see?" I asked.

"I blew my nose in a tissue. It was so yucky I couldn't use it again." She looked over her shoulder, just in case someone was listening. "When I tried to put the tissue in the bin, Mr Badal grabbed it and said he'd bin it for me."

Gross! I hated touching other people's dirty tissues.

"Anything else happen?" I asked.

"Um, when I needed to sharpen my colouring pencil, he wouldn't let me do it over the bin. He made me do it on a clean tissue. He put it all in the bin when I was done."

"That's weird…"

"There's more," she said. "When I got up to leave, he rushed over to the bin and pulled out the bin bag. He muttered something about Mrs Cherry. Then he tied a knot in the bag and put it by the door…The bag wasn't there today."

Mr Badal and Mrs Cherry were definitely keeping secrets. This wasn't a nice secret like a surprise school pet. This secret had to be bad. Why else was Mrs Cherry crying so much?

"Let's find that bin bag," I said. "Come on!"

I grabbed her hand and pulled her into the playground. We had to hurry before anyone came out!

There was a massive bin outside the kitchen's back door. Libby and I had to hold our noses as we got closer. The smell was more stinky than the school toilets.

The bin was packed full of small bin bags, green recycling bags and large black bags.

"Can you see Mr Badal's bin bag?" I asked. My voice sounded funny because I was pinching my nose.

Libby shook her head.

Oh boy, I thought. The bin bag might be deep down inside the massive bin. That means I have to…Yuck!

"If I fall in there, pull me out!" I told Libby. "Or get Jamar to help."

I grabbed the dirty bin and pulled myself up. The smell was so strong my eyes were watery. But I held on. I had to. I couldn't let Malcolm down.

"What did the bin bag look like?" I asked.

"It was white."

The massive bin was full of white bin bags. I needed more info to find Mr Badal's bin bag.

"How big was it?"

"Like the bin bag we have in class."

There were eight bags the same size as the one in class. I couldn't go through each one. I needed more info.

"You said Mr Badal tied a knot in the bag?"

"Yes," she said. "A very pretty one. It was a…a…a bow! Like the one I wore in my hair last week."

Tucked in a corner was a small, white bin bag. The top was tied in a pretty bow. I reached over and pulled it out.

It felt good being back on the ground. My hands were dirty and my white shirt had marks on it, but it was worth it. I could clean up after school before Dad saw me.

I tore open the bin bag and pulled rubbish out, bit by bit. I felt icky all over, but someone had to do it!

First, I pulled out some used tissues. Libby said sorry for the snotty one she'd used.

Second, I took out some old newspapers. Mr Badal was very naughty for putting them in the bin. They were supposed to be recycled. If he wasn't the headteacher, I would have told him off!

Finally, after taking out pencil shavings, ripped up letters and socks with holes in them, I got to the bottom of the bag.

I couldn't believe what I saw...

Chapter 17

In Mr Badal's bin bag was a small, plastic container. It was the perfect size for a hamster. I lifted off the top and found cotton wool bedding inside. Tucked away underneath was a chocolate hamster treat.

It was just like the ones I gave Malcolm.

"That's Malcolm's bedroom, isn't it?" Libby whispered. "And his bed. And his treat."

I didn't know what to say or do.

So, I just cried.

Libby gave me a big hug and wiped away

my tears. Then she gave me another hug and didn't let go.

"Why did they throw out Malcolm's bed?" I sobbed. "Why did they take him away?"

"I don't know but…" Libby bit her lip and looked away.

"It's okay," I said. "You can tell me."

Libby turned and pointed at the roof. I looked up and couldn't see anything special. There was the roof, a football someone had kicked up there, and…the security camera!

Years ago, Mr Badal bought lots of security cameras. They were in the playground, in the corridors and at the school gates. He said he got the cameras to keep us safe.

Actually, he got them because someone kept stealing his muffins. He wanted cameras so he could see who the muffin thief was.

It wasn't me…

"If we check the cameras," I said, "we'll know who put Malcolm's things in the bin."

"I don't think that's a good idea…"

"How can we check the cameras?" I asked. "I want to know who put this in the bin. It could be the same person who stole Malcolm!"

"Mr Badal probably dumped the bin after I left his office."

She could be right, but I had to be 100% sure. That's why I needed to see who was on the security camera.

"Libby, I think someone dumped Malcolm's things because they bought him new stuff. They want to keep him and make him *their* hamster."

"But he's *ours*," she cried. "They can't just steal someone's pet. That's wrong!"

"Don't worry," I said. "They won't get away with it."

"But how can we stop them? We don't even know who *they* are."

"The security cameras know," I said. "They record everything and save it on video. We can watch the videos if we know where they are."

"They're in Mr Badal's office. The videos play on a little television near his desk." Libby's voice started trembling when she spoke again. "He's very fussy about people going into his offices. We can't just walk in there."

Mr Badal had *two* offices because he liked buying new stuff for himself. He had two desks, two chairs, two laptops, two mobiles and two lots of everything else.

I didn't think it was fair. We only had one classroom. Why did he have two offices?

"Libby, we must see the security camera videos."

"But they're in Mr Badal's office."

"I know…"

We were going into Mr Badal's office. As long as he didn't catch us watching the security videos, everything would be fine.

What if he *did* catch us? Hopefully we'd just get detention for a few days. Maybe we'd get suspended from school for a week or two.

But if Mr Badal was in a really, really bad mood, we wouldn't get detention or suspension. We'd be expelled. Expulsion means we'd be banned from school not for days, weeks or even months, but forever…

Chapter 18

The bell rang. Lunchtime was over. Everyone else went out to play, but Jamar, Libby and I stayed in. We waited by the toilets until the corridor was empty.

"Is everyone ready?" Jamar asked, his voice trembling. "Just stick to the plan, okay?"

The plan was simple, but it wouldn't be easy.

Libby would keep Mr Badal busy while Jamar and I looked around his office. Jamar said we shouldn't look in anything top secret, but everything else was okay.

"No snooping on his computer," Jamar told me, "and no looking through the filing cabinets."

"No fair!" I cried.

"Too bad," he said.

Libby was shaking. I held her hand and it was really sweaty.

"It's okay," I said. "If we get caught, Mr Badal won't know you helped us."

"But I..." When Libby saw Jamar watching her, she froze.

"I get nervous too sometimes," he said. "Just stop and take a deep breath."

Libby took a very deep breath. She kept her eyes away from Jamar when she spoke again.

"I'm not worried about me," she said softly. "I'm worried about *you*."

"Sometimes police officers have to do scary things," Jamar said. "It's just part of the job."

"But making Mr Badal angry is a *very* scary thing," Libby said. "I'm scared you two will get into BIG trouble."

"Jamar and I are scared too, but we've got to do something or we'll never see Malcolm again." I closed my eyes and imagined Malcolm's fluffy, fat cheeks stuffed with food. "I miss him so much."

"I miss him too," Libby said, teary-eyed. "He was so fuzzy and soft."

"We'll see him again soon," I said. "We'll check the cameras and find out who took him. Then we'll get him back!"

"You're right," Libby said, smiling a little. "The hamster thief won't get away with this!"

We followed Jamar to Mr Badal's office. Just standing outside the door made my legs wobble and palms sweaty.

Before Jamar knocked, he pulled out a

drink bottle. Inside was chunky soup.

"What's the soup for?" I asked.

"A back-up in case things go wrong," he said. "A good police officer always has a back-up plan."

"What's the back-up plan?"

"You'll drink this and…Never mind. I'm sure you won't need to."

"Need to what?"

"Never mind!"

He put the bottle of soup into my lunchbox.

"When I tell you to drink it, drink it."

"But why?"

"You'll see."

Jamar knocked on the door. Heavy footsteps stomped closer and closer. Then Mr Badal gave a very, very loud sigh.

The door flew open.

Mr Badal towered over us. He gave me a

mean look, gave Libby a friendly smile, and then pulled Jamar inside.

Libby didn't move.

"Come in, Libby," Mr Badal said. "You're always welcome here...Your friend can enter too."

Libby and I followed them in.

"Jamar, my boy! What a pleasure to see you again!" Mr Badal pulled out a chair for Jamar to sit down. Libby and I squashed into the other seat.

Mr Badal rushed around the desk to his own chair. It was so huge it made him look small. His finger slipped down the armrest and pushed a button. The chair started humming.

"The vibration function is just what I need at lunchtime," Mr Badal said happily. "Jamar, I am so glad I listened to you!"

"Listened to him?" I asked.

"What's your name again?" Mr Badal asked. "Melissa? Miranda? Megan?"

"Mya Dove."

"Never heard of you," Mr Badal mumbled. "Well, Mya, Jamar gave invaluable feedback on my new office. He has a great eye for the finest details."

"The office looks great," Jamar said. "When I grow up, I want an office just like this one."

I took a good look around. The place didn't look that special to me. The walls were all bland brown. The carpet was the same colour as mud.

There were only two things I liked in Mr Badal's office. One was the pretty map of India on the wall. It was painted in gold and silver with a black frame.

The second nice thing in his office was his comfy-looking leather chair. Our plastic chair was so hard it hurt my bum. Sitting on the floor would've been more comfortable.

Mr Badal's desk was huge. He had piles of papers and folders everywhere. On the windowsill were thick books. They must've been very heavy to hold.

In a corner were two big filing cabinets with four drawers each. Sitting on top of the furthest cabinet was a tiny television.

He watches the cameras on that, I thought to myself. But where is the remote control?

"Young lady!" Mr Badal snapped at me. "It is *very* rude to stare!"

I hung my head in shame.

"So, Jamar, how can I assist you today?" Mr Badal gave a big smile. "I always have time for the best Prefect there is."

"Sir, Libby said she can't find her colouring pencils."

Libby nodded, not looking Mr Badal in

the eye.

"She wondered if they might be in the staff room."

"I'll have Mandy look as soon as possible."

Mandy was the receptionist. She was so lovely and sweet. Nothing like mean Mr Badal.

"Could you check the staff room now?" Jamar asked. "We'd appreciate it."

"I would love to, but I have so much work to do." Mr Badal frowned. "There are so many naughty children. I must write letters to their parents. If only every student was as well-mannered as you and Libby."

Mr Badal looked down his nose at me.

"Is there anything else I can do for you or are we finished here?"

"Is that a new television?" Jamar asked, pointing at the tiny television on the filing cabinet.

"It's a monitor, not a television," Mr Badal said. "It's the best camera monitor in the world today. I can see every single security camera at the exact same time."

"That's so cool," Jamar cried. "I'd love to see that."

"Jamar, you just had to ask!"

Mr Badal turned on the security camera monitor. It was a tiny television that showed what each camera saw.

First the monitor showed the corridor cameras. Suddenly it switched to the playground cameras. Then it changed to the cameras at the back gate. I could see some lucky kids going home early.

"Why does it keep changing like that?" I asked. "It's annoying!"

"No, it is NOT," Mr Badal hissed. "The cameras have modern technology called motion detection. They spot even the tiniest movement and record it...If anyone dares to enter my office and steal my muffins, I'll know before they devour the first crumb!"

"Good for you!" Jamar cried. "I don't like people who steal muffins. Just get your own!"

Mr Badal nodded in agreement.

"So, children, if there is nothing else to discuss then I must return to my heavy workload. Redecorating my offices took its toll on me. I deserve another holiday."

"But I'd love to see the cameras again," Jamar said quickly. "Do they record every day? How long are the videos saved for?"

"They record all day every single day of the year. Recordings are kept for sixty days before deletion. Isn't that wonderful?"

Mr Badal stood up and waved us out of his office. He barely looked at me before turning to Libby.

"You're doing so well," he said to her. "I'm

proud of you. I knew you could make friends."

Then Mr Badal turned to Jamar.

"You should redecorate my upstairs office too," Mr Badal said. "You're the best decorator I know. I can't believe you're only eleven!"

"Sir, I have a history project due in seven days." Jamar pulled a sad face. "Maybe you could put in a good word with Mr Hardy? With an extension, I would have enough time to help you."

"Is a week-long extension sufficient?"

Jamar smiled. "It will have to do."

We stepped outside the office and Mr Badal closed the door behind us.

"That didn't work!" I said. "What should we do now?"

"Remember the bottle of chunky soup I gave you? Drink it but don't swallow! Just hold it in your mouth."

I couldn't argue with Jamar, the Chief Superintendent, just like the teachers didn't argue with Mr Badal. Sometimes you must do what your boss says.

I drank the soup and held it in my mouth. My cheeks puffed out, just like Malcolm's used to when he ate too much.

"Hold it, Mya," Jamar said. "Don't worry. It'll be worth it, I promise!"

I gave him a thumbs up.

"Libby?" Jamar turned to her. "You'd better go now. Thanks for telling us about the bin bag. You've been a big help."

"I…I'm…" Libby stepped closer to Jamar so he could hear her quiet voice. "I'm not going. We're a team. I'm staying to the end."

"Well, you'd better stand back," he said. "You don't wanna get hit!"

"Hit by what?" she asked.

He looked at me. "You'll see."

Jamar grabbed me by the shoulders and spun me around really fast. At first my eyes were open and everything was a blur. Then I closed my eyes, but that didn't stop me from feeling dizzy.

Faster and faster he spun me until I felt sick. Then he let go and I almost fell over. My thoughts were jumbled in my brain. I could barely think straight.

"Mr Badal, come quick!" Jamar cried.

The door flew open and Jamar helped me inside. Mr Badal stood back, his eyes wide open in fear.

"What's wrong with her?" Mr Badal asked.

"She's feeling sick," Jamar said. "I think the flu is going around Year Four."

"Well, keep it away from me and my office!" Mr Badal kicked over the bin. "Let her do what she needs to in there."

Libby held my hair back when I leaned over the bin.

"Spit the soup onto the floor," Jamar whispered. "Hurry!"

I opened my mouth and the soup sprayed out. Because Jamar spun me around so fast, it wasn't just soup that came out...

Chapter 19

Mr Badal fell onto his chair and closed his eyes. He breathed quickly and started trembling. Libby went over and fanned him with some papers off his desk. Jamar stayed with me, patting my back.

Suddenly Mr Badal jumped off his chair and ran around the desk to me.

"You poor thing," he cried. "Don't worry! I'll make it all better, I promise!"

"I'm okay—"

"Not you," he snapped at me. "I'm talking to my poor little carpet. Do you know how much she cost? The poor darling."

Mr Badal grabbed his phone and tapped the numbers quickly. Then he returned to his chair and Libby started fanning him again.

"Hello? Get the cleaner on the phone immediately!" Mr Badal stopped to take a deep breath. "Is this the cleaner? Good! Get to my downstairs office this instant. It is a code red! No, silly woman. Sick on my carpet, and a lot of it."

He slammed the phone down and wheeled his chair away from us.

"Save yourself, Mr Badal," Jamar cried. "I don't want you catching the flu too!"

"Jamar, you're a star!" Mr Badal edged out of the room, keeping as far away from me as he could. "I *am* the headteacher, after all. I cannot catch the flu and take sick leave. Without me, the school will fall apart. It would be like a ship without a captain. Who will steer the ship? Who will guide the crew?"

"You'd better get going," Jamar said. "Now I'm feeling a bit sick too…"

Mr Badal ran out the office and didn't look back.

The three of us sighed with relief. Mr Badal was finally gone, but the cleaners would be here soon. We had to hurry!

"The camera monitor must have a remote control," Jamar said. "Find it!"

We opened the drawers and cabinets, searching quickly for the remote control. It was hard to find because Mr Badal had so much stuff. Every drawer was packed full of books, folders, papers, pens and pencils.

Suddenly Libby stopped and held up a remote control. She pointed it at the camera monitor and the screen flashed.

"Good girl," Jamar said, taking the remote. "Let's check every video since

Malcolm went missing. We'll see who put the bin bag outside."

Jamar rewound the tape for what seemed like forever. The cameras recorded EVERYTHING outside. Even when a leaf blew across the playground, the camera recorded it.

"Wait, go back," Libby said quietly. "I think I saw someone with the bin bag."

Jamar rewound and pressed play. We gathered around the tiny monitor and leaned in for a closer look.

The playground door opened and someone peeked out. The person was wearing a black, baggy hoodie. They kept the hood pulled over their face as they crossed the playground. Tucked under their arm was a plastic bag with the handles tied in a bow.

"That's the bin bag from Mr Badal's office," I said. "This person dumped it in the massive bin outside the kitchen."

The playground door swung open and two boys ran out, playfighting. The hooded person slipped behind the massive bin and hid there until the boys went back inside.

When the playground was empty, the hooded person tiptoed over to the bin and opened it. They held their nose while they dumped the bin bag.

That's when we spotted the second plastic bag they were holding.

"That looks like the plastic bag Mrs Cherry had on Wednesday," I said. "I think Mr Badal told her to get rid of it."

Was the sneaky, hooded person Mrs Cherry? Or was it Mr Badal?

Next, the hooded person reached up to dump the second bin bag...but they didn't. Instead, they slipped it into their pocket and rushed back into school.

By switching through the cameras, we watched the person walk down the corridor. They stopped outside Mr Murphy the caretaker's room.

The hooded person slipped into Mr Murphy's room and stayed there for five minutes.

"I wish there was a camera in there," Jamar said. "Never mind. The person is coming out now."

The hooded person came out, but they weren't holding the plastic bag anymore. Empty-handed, the person went into the adults' toilets. Those toilets were only for Mr Badal, teachers, Mr Murphy, Mandy, cleaners and dinner ladies. No students allowed, not even Prefects.

"Go back to Mr Murphy's room," I said. "The person left the bag there."

Jamar pressed the remote and the monitor

switched back to Mr Murphy's door.

Mr Murphy stepped out of his room. He had a shovel in one hand and the plastic bag in the other. He looked over his shoulder suspiciously before sneaking outside.

"Mr Murphy is in on this too," I cried. "So that's Mr Badal, Mrs Cherry and Mr Murphy. What are they hiding?"

The caretaker crept outside, trying hard to stay off camera. It didn't work, though. When one camera couldn't see him, another one could.

Mr Murphy crossed the playground and stopped beside the tree. He started digging at the roots, only stopping to wipe his sweaty forehead.

"I'll stop the video here," Jamar said, his face turning pale. "I don't think we should watch anymore."

"No," I cried. "I want to see what he's

burying."

"I'm sorry, Mya." Jamar looked very sad. "I wasn't sure if Mrs Gable was right earlier, but now I know she was…"

I grabbed the remote and fast forwarded.

Soon the hole had been dug and Mr Murphy was holding the plastic bag over it. He bowed his head for a moment, and then placed the bag in the hole. Quickly, he covered the bag with dirt.

"What's he doing now?" I asked.

Mr Murphy rushed to the daisies on the windowsill and took the biggest one. He went back to the tree and placed the flower on top of the bag he'd buried.

Knock knock.

That wasn't the video. That was someone outside Mr Badal's office. We'd run out of time!

"It's the cleaners," Jamar whispered. "We

need to go!"

"No," I said. "I want to know who was in that hoodie."

"Mya—"

"No, Jamar. I'm not giving up on Malcolm."

"Mya, we need to talk."

"About what?"

Knock knock.

"About Malcolm," he said. "There's something you need to know…"

Knock knock.

"But not right now," he said. "Mya, go clean up. You smell really bad!"

The cleaner looked surprised when we opened the door. I held my stomach and pretended to feel sick. Libby stayed behind us, keeping her eyes to the floor.

I didn't want to stop looking for Malcolm, but Jamar was right – I smelt really bad. I had to hold my nose just so I couldn't smell myself. There was no way I'd go back to class smelling like that.

And I couldn't go home smelling like that either. My mum wouldn't be very happy about it…

"Should we meet up at breaktime?" I asked.

"No," Jamar said quickly. "I need to talk to my dad about something first. It's hard to explain to younger kids…"

Jamar walked away, his head down. He wasn't crying but it looked like he might soon.

"Mya, I feel scared for Malcolm," Libby whispered. "I think something bad happened to him…"

"Don't worry, Libby," I said, patting her on the back. "We'll see Malcolm again soon."

Very soon, actually…

Chapter 20

On Friday morning, Mrs Cherry skipped around the classroom like someone *my* age! She was cracking jokes and laughing, too. I hadn't seen her smile so much in days!

"Good morning, class!" she said. "Isn't today a great day?"

Everyone looked confused. No one said anything.

"Let's play some beautiful music!"

Mrs Cherry opened the store cupboard and took out musical instruments. Everyone tried to grab one, but I didn't. I couldn't stop looking at Malcolm's empty cage.

"Mya, what would you like to play today?" Mrs Cherry asked. "There's still the harmonica left."

I covered my ears to keep out the noise. There were bongo drums thumping and cymbals crashing. Jimmy played the guitar like a rock star. Angel hogged the violin so no one else could play it. Her friends were so bad at singing, they sounded like cats fighting over the last piece of tuna.

"I don't want to play anything," I said. "I'm not feeling well."

"I hope you aren't coming down with the flu too." Mrs Cherry put her hand on my forehead. Then she placed her fingers on my wrist and checked how fast my heart was going. "I'm no doctor, but you seem just fine to me."

She gave me the harmonica. I played it

until she walked away. Then I put it down and rested my head on the desk.

"What a lovely day it is," Mrs Cherry said. "I can't wait for our special guest to show up."

"Who's the special guest?" I asked.

"It's a surprise!" She put a finger to her lips. "I can't ruin the surprise, can I? You'll just have to wait until later. I know *you* will be very happy when you see him."

Mrs Cherry started typing away on her computer. She laughed but didn't share the joke.

"Who's the guest?" Libby whispered in my ear.

"No idea," I said. "I know what she's doing and I'm not falling for it!"

Mrs Cherry, Mr Badal and Mr Murphy were all keeping secrets. They knew where Malcolm was. They'd dumped his things. All we had was his empty cage. For some reason, today she'd refilled his water bottle and food bowl.

But she knew he wasn't coming back.

Mrs Cherry had taken Malcolm for herself. I just knew it. She loved him so much that she'd taken him home.

But that wasn't fair!

Malcolm was a school pet, not a teacher's pet. He loved everyone at school, not just Mrs Cherry.

I wasn't the only one who missed Malcolm. Jamar, Libby, Jimmy, and everyone else in class missed him too.

I won't let her steal our pet, I thought. I have to do something!

I thought of the sneaky, hooded person on video yesterday. I couldn't remember seeing any teachers wearing a hoodie at school.

"Libby," I whispered, "why do people

wear hoodies?"

"My dad wears it when he goes for a run. He said it keeps him warm."

"It was a bit cold on Wednesday but not inside. Why did that person wear their hood up indoors?"

"To hide from the cameras."

"We've got to find out who wore that hoodie," I said. "If people wear it because it's cold then…"

I looked at all the closed windows.

If it got cold inside, the person with the hoodie might put it on. I thought the hooded person was Mrs Cherry. I just had to prove it.

"Mrs Cherry!" I cried. "Can you come here, please?"

She rushed over with a smile.

"Glad you're feeling better," she said. "Have you enjoyed *looking* at the harmonica, Mya? You'd enjoy *playing* it even more."

"Miss, I was sick yesterday."

"Why didn't you say something sooner?" she asked. "Are you all right?"

"Don't worry about me, I'm just fine." I pointed at the windows. "Could we open the windows, please? My mum said fresh air is healthy."

"I think we should keep the windows closed," she said. "It's been a bit cold this week."

I pulled a sad face and gave her puppy dog eyes. It worked. She knelt down and took my hand.

"What's wrong, Mya?"

"I wanted the windows open for some fresh air. I thought the fresh air would take my cold away so someone else doesn't catch it." I looked right in her eyes and said, "I got the cold from you, you know? I don't want to make someone else sick like you made me sick."

"Sorry about that," she said sadly. "I caught the cold from Malcolm's previous owner."

Mrs Cherry's white cheeks turned bright pink. She hurried off to open the windows.

"Now we wait," I whispered to Libby.

It took twenty minutes, but soon the classroom felt really cold. Some people complained, but Mrs Cherry told them fresh air was good for us.

"Any minute now," I told Libby. "Let it get a bit colder…"

Five minutes later, the sun went behind the clouds. It was dark outside and got even colder inside.

"I think that's enough time," I said to Libby. "You ready?"

She nodded.

"Mrs Cherry, can we close the windows

now? Libby's sniffing!"

Mrs Cherry rushed around class, closing the windows. When she walked past, she had tiny goose bumps on her arms. That meant she was cold too, but when she got back to her desk, she didn't put a jumper or hoodie on. She just sat there rubbing her arms.

"Miss," I said, "aren't you cold?"

"I'm just warming myself up," she replied. "I'll be fine in a few minutes. Libby, are you all right? Mya said you were sniffing. I'd hate to give you my cold too."

Libby was still too scared to speak in front of everybody, so her eyes lowered to the desk and she said nothing.

"What'd you say, Libby?" I asked, pretending Libby had said something. "You feel really, really cold now? Oh well. I wish we had a BIG jumper to give you. Then you'd be nice and warm and wouldn't get

Mrs Cherry's cold."

Mrs Cherry's eyes fell behind her desk. There was something on her bag, but I couldn't see it from my desk.

"Poor you, Libby!" I cried. "I wish I could give you a jumper or HOODIE, but I don't have one…Does anyone else?"

Several people put their hands up, but I waved them all back down.

"Thanks but no thanks," I said quickly. "We need a bigger jumper. Big jumpers keep us warm longer than small ones. It'd be nice to have a HOODIE so Libby's head could be warm too."

Mrs Cherry reached behind her desk and pulled out a plastic bag. She turned it over and a dark hoodie fell out. It looked just like the black, baggy hoodie from the security camera video.

Libby's mouth gaped open.

So did mine.

Mrs Cherry brought over the hoodie and helped Libby put it on.

"Do you feel better now?" Mrs Cherry asked. "Everyone, please put your jumpers on. The fresh air was a bit too cold. Apologies!"

Mrs Cherry skipped back to her desk and opened a book. There was a hamster on the cover.

Why's she reading about hamsters? I wondered. Probably because she's taking care of Malcolm at her house.

"Can you smell that?" Libby whispered. "The hoodie smells familiar."

When Mrs Cherry turned away, I quickly sniffed the hoodie's sleeve. It smelt familiar to me too.

I closed my eyes and thought long and hard. Where had I smelt that smell before? At home when we'd repainted my bedroom. It used to be a boring beige colour. Now it was golden yellow, just like my police badge.

"My room smelt like that when we painted it," I said. "It's the smell of paint. It goes away after a while, but you need to open some windows first."

Libby looked over the hoodie and stopped under her elbow. I turned the sleeve so I could get a closer look.

There was a patch of white paint. I tried scrubbing it off but it was dry. Dry paint is very hard to get off clothes. I felt sorry for the person who did Mrs Cherry's washing.

I put my hand up.

"Mrs Cherry, why is there paint on your hoodie?"

Libby held up her arm to show the stain.

Mrs Cherry didn't look very happy anymore. She rushed over and took a closer look at the paint mark.

"When on earth did this happen?" she asked herself. "Oh, I remember. Mr Murphy's office…"

"Mr Murphy? Why did you go to see him?" I asked.

"Oh, um, well, um, you see…I took him a birthday card."

She had a bulky plastic bag in the video. I hadn't seen anything that looked like a card. That meant she was fibbing. I liked her, so I gave her a chance to tell the truth.

"Did you buy him a present?"

"No, just a card."

"Nothing else at all. Not even a present you'd have to carry in a plastic bag?"

Her eyes narrowed. "What makes you say that?"

Oh no, I thought. I asked too many questions. She's suspicious!

"I want to get him a present too," I said. "I don't want to get him the same thing as you."

"I'm sure he's got enough presents, so don't trouble yourself." Mrs Cherry looked happy again. "Well, back to music, you two!"

"Mrs Cherry, can I write a song?"

"Of course! Songwriting is an important part of music."

When Mrs Cherry went back to her desk, I took out a pen and paper. She thought I was writing a song. Actually, I was writing down proof that Mrs Cherry had stolen Malcolm.

"Will you take the proof to your secret boss?" Libby whispered.

"Not yet," I said. "I want to be sure before I say anything to the Children's Police Force."

"Are you going to arrest Mrs Cherry by yourself?" Libby asked, her eyes widening.

"Will your handcuffs fit her big wrists?"

"Yes, and yes. I tried the handcuffs on my dad when he forgot his wedding anniversary. My mum let me do it because she was very angry with him."

"But…I like Mrs Cherry." Libby wiped a tear from her eye. "She's been so nice to me."

Libby was right. Mrs Cherry was a great teacher. She'd taught us so much cool stuff. One time she showed us how to split light into rainbow colours. Another time we got to grow cress seeds. I liked eating them afterwards!

Mrs Cherry was a nice teacher, but stealing Malcolm wasn't a nice thing to do. He was the school pet. He belonged to everyone, not just her.

"I have to put her in detention," I said. "I don't want to, but I have to."

"Could you let her go? Just this once?"

Libby begged. "Please? She's the nicest teacher I've ever had. Other ones were mean to me because I'm quiet."

"I won't let her get away with stealing Malcolm," I said. "She doesn't let us get away with being naughty, does she?"

"Let's talk to Jamar first. Please? He wanted to talk about something."

"Okay, I'll wait."

A part of me was happy about waiting. I didn't want to put Mrs Cherry in detention. I'd happily put Mr Badal and Angel in detention, but not Mrs Cherry.

Too bad, I thought. She's a very naughty teacher and needs to be told off.

My plan was simple. Talk to Jamar, come back to class, handcuff Mrs Cherry and take her straight to detention. She might cry a little, but it was her own fault for being so naughty.

She'll be very surprised when I arrest her, I thought. The whole class will be shocked too.

What I didn't know was that Mrs Cherry had a trick up her sleeve. It was something nobody in class saw coming. Something that would turn the whole case upside down...

Chapter 21

At morning breaktime, Libby and I met Jamar outside the Year Six classroom. He still looked sad about yesterday.

"Come on, girls," he said. "We'll talk outside."

We followed him to the playground. He glanced at the tree before turning away. He didn't want to go there, but I definitely did!

I rushed to the tree. It looked just as Mr Murphy left it. The pretty daisy was still lying on the dirt.

"Let's dig it up," I said. "We'll find out

what he buried!"

"No way!" Jamar shouted. "We can't do that."

"Why not?" I asked.

"Because it's…" Jamar turned from me to Libby. "Libby, do you get what's down there? You figured out what he buried?"

She shook her head.

"Haven't your parents talked to you about…you know."

"We don't know what you're on about," I said. "Just tell us."

"You'd better sit down first," he said.

We all sat under the tree. Jamar put his arm around us and took a deep breath before speaking.

"Libby, Mya, I have something to tell you. It's about Malcolm."

"What about him?" I asked.

"Malcolm is…" He pointed up. "He's up

there."

"In the tree?" Libby asked. "Why is he up there?"

"No, I mean up there!"

He pointed at the sky.

"Jamar," I said, "he can't be up there. Hamsters can't fly."

I placed my hand on his forehead. My mum did that to check if I was sick. He didn't feel too hot or too cold. He felt okay, not sick at all.

"Girls, um, I hate to tell you this but…"

Jamar looked from me to Libby to me to Libby again. He opened his mouth to speak. No words came out. He closed his mouth and looked to the sky again.

"Girls, you remember how Malcolm got the flu? The flu is a very bad cold. Well, poor Malcolm got sicker and sicker until he—"

Mrs Cherry blew the whistle. She skipped

around the playground, stopping to speak to people from our class. They looked much happier after speaking to her.

After she spoke to Jimmy, he ran right over to us. Hopping about, he wouldn't keep still.

"What's going on?" I asked.

"Guess what?" he cried. "Malcolm is back!"

"No way!" Jamar sprung up and looked Jimmy right in the eye. "Are you telling fibs?"

"Malcolm is back. He's in class," Jimmy said. "Mrs Cherry just told us."

I couldn't believe it! After all this time looking for him, Malcolm had come back on his own.

I should've been happy, but I wasn't. I was *very* angry with him. We'd been so worried, and I'd been through so much! I could've been locked in Year Six's store cupboard forever! I'd dug in a dirty, stinky bin with my bare hands! I'd been sick on Mr Badal's brand-new carpet!

It could have been much worse. What if I'd tried to arrest Mrs Cherry for stealing Malcolm? It would've been embarrassing when he showed up! I would've been wrong in front of the whole class.

I stormed across the playground and lined up with our class. While everyone else chatted about Malcolm, I kept to myself.

When I see his cute little face again, I thought, I'm going to give him a piece of my mind!

Now we all thought the mystery had been solved. Malcolm was back. Mrs Cherry was happy. Everything would go back to normal.

But when we got upstairs, things wouldn't go back to normal. Instead, everything would change forever…

Chapter 22

Everyone was quiet. All eyes were on Mrs Cherry. She was by the windowsill where Malcolm's cage sat. It was covered with a thin, white sheet.

"Is everyone ready?" Mrs Cherry asked.

We nodded.

"Are you sure?"

I could hear Malcolm's wheel spinning faster and faster. Soon he was running so fast the whole cage trembled. That had never happened before.

"Boys and girls, I'd like you to

meet…again…Malcolm!"

Mrs Cherry pulled off the sheet and stepped back. Everyone rushed over to the cage, struggling to see over people's heads. I squeezed round the side for a closer look.

There he was. Malcolm. The same glossy fur, the same bright eyes, the same cute paws and even cuter feet.

He looked up at me and stared.

I smiled at him.

He turned away.

"Class, calm down," Mrs Cherry said. "Malcolm is tired. He went on a long trip and just arrived back this morning."

"Where did he go?" I asked.

"Probably to see his previous owner," she replied. "He missed her so much."

Malcolm looked around at everyone. He ran up the tiny stairs and stood on his back legs. He reached up and grabbed the bars on top of his cage. Soon he was swinging on them like they were monkey bars.

"Everyone, please take your seats," Mrs Cherry said. "This is an English lesson, remember?"

Nobody moved.

"Boys and girls, back to your seats!" Mrs Cherry stood, hands on hips. "I will bring Malcolm around the class so he can say hello."

We returned to our seats. Everyone, even Libby, looked happy to see Malcolm. But they weren't just looking at him. They were also looking at me.

Some people gave me funny looks. Some people even laughed at me.

"Mya said Malcolm was missing," someone whispered.

"She said Year Six stole him," another person said. "Nobody stole him! He just went away for a bit."

Jimmy gently nudged me in the arm and leaned in to talk.

"Mya, it's okay," he said. "Every police officer makes mistakes sometimes."

"I know but...I don't like to get things wrong." I blinked back tears, my face feeling hot. "It's *so* embarrassing!"

My face was burning from shame. And I felt guilty. I'd made everyone worry for nothing. Malcolm was just fine.

One by one, everyone got to give Malcolm a quick hug and talk to him. Usually he'd sit still and listen, but not today. Now he wouldn't stop moving. He kept trying to climb down and run away. Luckily Mrs Cherry caught him in time.

Finally, it was my turn to hold him.

"Hello, Malcolm," I said quietly. "Why did you run off like that? Did you miss your old mummy?"

He looked away.

"I guess you don't feel like talking."

He started cleaning his face.

Now that I was holding Malcolm, I could take a closer look at him. I hoped he hadn't hurt himself on his trip.

His eyes looked brighter and wider than before. He'd started keeping his nails short and clean. I was glad his nose wasn't runny anymore, and was very happy he wasn't sneezing or coughing. It looked like the flu had gone.

He was back to normal.

"Time to say goodbye," Mrs Cherry said. "You can help me tidy his cage at breaktime."

"Yes, please!"

When Mrs Cherry held out her hand, Malcolm ran right on to it. Usually he'd stay on my hand until I gave him away. Not this time. It looked like he couldn't wait to leave me.

Like he didn't love me anymore.

A moment later, Malcolm was back in his cage. His cheeks were stuffed with food, so he took some out for a snack.

"Class, today we'll read some exciting new poems." Mrs Cherry held up a thick book of poetry. "Let's start with a fantasy poem! You'll love this one…"

Mrs Cherry started reading us a poem about a dragon slayer. She said we could write our own poems later in class.

I was very excited about hearing poems, and even more excited about writing them, but…something didn't feel right. Something about *Malcolm* didn't feel right.

Malcolm had the same hair, same eyes, same hands, same feet, but something about him was…*different*. His trip had changed him. Or maybe it was the bad cold he caught.

I also wondered about what Jamar was trying to tell us earlier. Why had he pointed to the clouds and said Malcolm was up there? Had Malcolm flown on a plane to his old owner? But how could he buy a plane ticket without any money?

Now Angel was staring at Malcolm's cage. She waved at him. He rested a paw on the cage and stared back at her. It was like they were best friends now. He used to be *my* best friend. Now he didn't seem to care about me at all.

Libby gently poked me in the arm, so I leaned over to hear her better.

"Do you have a tissue?" she asked. "I think Malcolm peed on my hand."

There was a tiny yellow stain on her palm. I gave her a tissue to wipe her hand.

When Mrs Cherry asked if anyone wanted

to hold Malcolm again, only Angel and her friends raised their hands.

"Nobody else?" Mrs Cherry asked. "Why don't the rest of you want to hold him?"

"Malcolm bit me," Jimmy said.

"No way," I said. "He *never* bites anyone but Angel. Probably because she's mean..."

"It wasn't a hard bite. Scared me more than anything."

"Sorry about that," Mrs Cherry said. "I'm sure Malcolm didn't mean to...Does anyone else want to hold him?"

"I'm not holding him again," Mark said. "He won't keep still!"

"He doesn't cuddle like he used to," Emma said sadly. "I missed him. He didn't miss me."

Mrs Cherry's face turned paper white.

"Class, Malcolm is extremely tired after his long trip. He travelled for hours there and back. When people are extremely tired, they can be a tad grouchy. He'll feel better soon."

"Miss," Emma said, "my grandparents travel around the whole world every year. They NEVER bite us when they get back."

"Well, I'd hope not," Mrs Cherry said. "But…remember he had the flu two days ago. He is still recovering. So am I."

"Miss," Jimmy said, "when my mum had the flu, she didn't pee on anybody. That's just gross!"

Everyone except Angel and her friends nodded in agreement.

"Miss," Jimmy continued, "Malcolm never peed on us before. Why's he doing it now?"

"I'm sure he has his reasons," Mrs Cherry said, her cheeks turning bright pink. "Angel, you can hold him first."

Angel held out her hands and Malcolm

ran on to them. He didn't bite her. He didn't pee on her. He didn't wriggle free. He just sat there happily, nibbling his food.

"What's everyone so upset about?" Angel snapped. "You're all just jealous because Malcolm loves me so much!"

She looked back and gave me the meanest look ever. Her narrow eyes were telling me something. Without speaking, she was saying, "I know something you don't know…" Her eyes went from me to Malcolm and back to me again.

That's when I knew the truth.

Malcolm looked the same but he was acting strangely. He hated Angel before. Now he loved her. He never bit or peed on anyone before. Now he kept doing it over and over. His eyes were brighter, bigger and wider than before. He wouldn't respond to his name anymore.

"Why's Malcolm acting so weird?" Jimmy asked.

"Because…" It was hard for me to say it. "Because, Jimmy, that hamster is *not* Malcolm…"

Chapter 23

"Class, listen carefully."

Mrs Cherry tapped a ruler on the whiteboard until everyone was quiet.

"Thank you. It's time for those lovely poems you've written. You don't have to, but it would be great if you read them out loud."

Angel put her hand up.

"Angel will go first," Mrs Cherry said. "Come on up!"

Angel rushed to the whiteboard and waved at everyone.

Nobody but her friends waved back.

"This is a brilliant, amazing, fantastic poem about…me," Angel said. "No talking while I'm speaking!"

Angel unfolded her paper and started reading her poem:

My name is Angel
Can't you see?
I am very, very
Very Pretty.

Everyone likes me
They love me too
It's not my fault
They don't like you.

All the girls are jealous of my hair

All the boys want to hold my
hand
All the teachers want to teach
me
Mr Badal likes to speak to me.

If you don't like this poem
I don't like you
If that makes you cry
Boo hoo hoo!

"Finished!" Angel cried, clapping for
herself. Her friends stood up and clapped so
loudly it made my ears hurt even more. My
ears already hurt because the poem was *so*
bad. I never wanted to hear it again!

"Excellent work," Mrs Cherry said. "Every
rhyme was magnificent."

"I know." Angel bowed. "Do I win anything?"

"No, dear. This isn't a competition." Mrs Cherry gently pushed Angel back to her seat. "Anyone else?"

I put my hand up.

"Come on over, Mya."

Libby grabbed my arm and pulled me closer. Her wide eyes stared down at my poem.

"Are you sure about this?" she asked. "I don't want you to get into trouble!"

"This is my job," I said. "Mrs Cherry won't get away with this. I won't let her!"

I stood up and marched down to the whiteboard. I didn't need to read my poem. I knew every word off by heart.

Last week Monday morning
We got a big surprise

A hamster called Malcolm
We couldn't believe our eyes.

Malcolm was cute
Cuddly too
He kept fit and healthy
Until he got the flu.

He got very sick
Like his old mummy
Didn't run anymore
Because it hurt his tummy.

On Wednesday everyone went
out to play
That's when poor Malcolm ran
away.

Mr Badal said get rid of it
That upset Mrs Cherry quite a
bit.

Mrs Cherry and Mrs Tipple
kept a secret
They talked in the corridor
Then went inside and closed
the door
They've never done that
before.

Mrs Cherry let me blame Year
Six
But really she was up to
tricks.
She took the hamster food I

hid in there

And left behind a dark red hair.

Mrs Cherry binned Malcolm's stuff

She wore a hoodie to look more rough

To reach Mr Murphy she had to creep around

And made him bury something in the playground.

Today she brings a hamster and he's mean

Peeing and biting everyone he's seen

Last week he hated Angel and
her friends
Now he can't wait to see them
again.

He looks the same as before
Smells the same too
Loves drinking water
And eating food too
But he's not Malcolm, can't you
see?
Mrs Cherry is trying to trick
you and me!

Everyone's jaw dropped. They all turned to
Mrs Cherry, who had tears in her eyes. She
stood up and tried to gently push me back to
my seat, but I wouldn't budge.

"Mya. Sit down. Now!"

"Mrs Cherry, tell the truth!" I cried. "He's not Malcolm. I know it. You know it. I bet Angel knows it too."

Everyone looked at Angel.

"Well, duh!" Angel said. "I never liked Malcolm anyway. Let's call this hamster Angelo. Angel and Angelo. I like that!"

"I don't care about Angelo," I said. "I want Malcolm back. Where is he?"

Mrs Cherry's eyes fell to the floor.

"Please," I begged. "Please…I just want to know he's okay."

"Take your seat, Mya," she said. "I have something very important to say…"

Mrs Cherry took my hand and led me back to my seat. I sat down, tears in my eyes. I could feel bad news coming soon.

Mrs Cherry sat down at her desk and took several deep breaths. She glanced at Angelo before looking across the room at me.

"Mya is correct," she said. "That is *not* Malcolm."

People gasped. Someone started crying. Angel sniggered. Her friends looked just as surprised as everyone else.

"Miss," I said, "you took Malcolm away. I have to arrest you."

Her eyes widened in shock.

"What have I done?" she asked.

"You have the right to be quiet. Anything you say will get you into trouble later. I'll be writing to your parents."

"You can't arrest me," she said calmly. "I haven't broken the law."

I got the plastic handcuffs from my rucksack and let everyone in class get a good look. Now they knew what would happen if they were naughty too.

"What am I being charged with?" Mrs

Cherry asked. She sat back and crossed her arms. "Which law have I broken?"

Oops! I hadn't done enough law research! I'd tried, but each law took hours to study. There were so many names, places and dates to remember!

"I'll choose a law later, okay?" I said, unlocking the handcuffs. "Put your hands behind your back. If you don't, I'll call your parents AND your grandparents."

"I have done nothing wrong. I made a mistake, sure, but nothing to be arrested for."

"We'll see about that!"

I turned to the class.

"Who was the last person to see Malcolm? Mrs Cherry! And probably Mr Badal too! Am I wrong, Miss?"

"No, I won't deny it because it's true. I was the last person to see Malcolm before he..."

She wiped a tear from her eye. I felt sorry for her, but a police officer has to do their job no matter what. She couldn't go around taking school pets. It was naughty!

"On Wednesday afternoon, is it true that Mr Badal said to you, "He, she, it. Get rid. Now." Did he say that?"

Her bright pink cheeks slowly turned as red as her hair.

"I heard him say it, so don't bother trying to dis...dis..."

"Discredit you?"

"Please, it's *very* rude to interrupt."

"Yes. That conversation happened on Wednesday afternoon in this room. He told me to get rid of...something."

"Get rid of what?" I asked.

"...Nothing."

"How do you get rid of nothing?"

"You can't," she said.

"Then you must've gotten rid of *something*, not nothing."

"I don't want to talk about this anymore," she said. "Next question, please!"

Mrs Cherry crossed her arms and frowned at me.

"Is it true that on Wednesday you had a runny nose like someone who has a cold?" I leaned in. "Didn't you tell me on Wednesday morning that Malcolm had a cold? You caught it when you tried to take him away!"

"I did not have a cold on Wednesday. My nose was runny because I was crying."

"Why cry? Marking tests isn't *that* boring, is it?"

"I was crying because..." She looked at the cage and started crying again.

"Because you feel guilty," I said. "Crocodile tears. I won't fall for it!"

I did feel very guilty about seeing her cry,

but a police officer must do their job. Besides, some people fake cry.

"What about the hamster food I left in the cupboard?" I asked.

"I put it in the bin," she replied. "I wanted you to think Malcolm was hiding in class somewhere."

"Is that the secret you were keeping with Mrs Tipple the other day?"

"Yes. And no." Mrs Cherry sank into her chair. "I told her what really happened to Malcolm. She told me to be honest with you all...I should've listened."

"And what about Mr Murphy? What did he bury the other day?"

"How did you find out about that?" she cried. "There was no one else around!"

"That's a secret," I said. "Now please answer my question. What did Mr Murphy bury under the tree?"

Mrs Cherry pulled out a tissue from her desk drawer and dabbed her eyes.

"Mrs Cherry stole Malcolm for herself," I said. "He's such an amazing pet that she wants him all for herself. She didn't get rid of him. She *stole* him. He's probably at her house right now."

"You're wrong."

"Then what really happened?" I asked. "If I'm wrong, what's right?"

"…You really want the truth?"

Everyone but Angel nodded. She didn't seem interested at all.

"Then I'll give you the truth. Mya, take your seat right now." She wiped her eyes with the tissue. "I have something important to announce, something I should have announced on Wednesday afternoon."

She stopped to wipe the tears on her cheeks and then took a very deep breath.

"Malcolm did not run away and I did not steal him," she said. "On Wednesday afternoon, I went to his cage and found him lying by his bed. When I reached down to stroke him, I realised something terrible had happened…"

Chapter 24

"Class, this is hard for me to say, but it must be done." Mrs Cherry gulped, her face covered in sweat. "Our dearest pet Malcolm…crossed over two days ago."

"Crossed over the road?" Emma asked.

"Crossed over the playground?" Jimmy asked.

"No, children, I mean…Malcolm passed on."

"Passed on human food?" Jimmy asked. "He didn't want my sandwiches either. He's a fussy eater."

"Or my juicy, red apple," Emma said. "It was a *very* tasty apple!"

"No, children, I mean Malcolm…went to sleep."

"Then let's wake him up!" I said. "Can we buy him an alarm? Is there an alarm for hamsters?"

"Wait a minute…" Jimmy said. "Do you mean he went to sleep or he went to SLEEP?"

"Same thing," Emma said.

"No, it's not." Jimmy's eyes lowered to his desk and stayed there. "My parents put my dog to sleep months ago…He never woke up."

"Why couldn't you wake him up?" I asked. "Did you try using an alarm, or turn the TV up really loud? That always wakes my brother up."

"This was different," Jimmy said. "When he closed his eyes to sleep, it was…*different*. I looked in his eyes and it felt like he was saying goodbye, not goodnight. He never woke up again."

"Sometimes we put pets to sleep," Mrs Cherry said. "It happens if they get really, really sick or old. They are in so much pain that it is KIND to put them to sleep. Then they get to rest forever. No more pain. Just a lovely, peaceful sleep."

"Will we sleep like that too?" Emma asked. "I want to wake up! I don't want to sleep forever."

"Only *very* sick people or animals pass away in their sleep. The rest of us wake up to enjoy another day."

Mrs Cherry was smiling through her tears. She wasn't the only one crying. Now other people were crying too.

"Malcolm went to sleep by himself," Mrs Cherry said. "It happened because he caught a cold from his previous owner. It was a very serious cold called pneumonia. Sadly, his little body could not handle it."

"He was moving slowly in the hamster ball," I said. "He wasn't eating much, but I thought he'd gone on a diet."

"Pneumonia can cause a loss of appetite," Mrs Cherry said. "That's why he stopped eating."

"He didn't like his food anymore?" I asked. "Maybe he would've eaten something if I'd brought him tastier hamster treats…but it's too late now. He's gone and it's all my fault."

"What? Mya, no!" Mrs Cherry cried. "Don't say that, sweetie."

"But it *is* my fault," I said. "I should've taken him to my mum. She's a nurse at the hospital. She would've made him better."

"Mya, his passing is *not* your fault. He got

very sick and passed away. It happens. *No one is to blame.*"

I didn't feel so guilty anymore, but I still felt sad. And confused. Had he really gone away *forever*?

"He couldn't recover from his illness," Mrs Cherry said. "Sometimes our pets get sick just like people do. Next time we'll keep a much closer eye on our pet and take him to the vet as soon as possible."

More and more people were crying, but I couldn't understand why. I did feel sad, but I wasn't sure why. Was Malcolm really *never* coming back?

"I don't get it," I said. "Malcolm crossed over? He passed on? He went to sleep? I don't get it!"

"Mya, you understand what happened, but it's very hard to accept it." Mrs Cherry said softly, "Malcolm died."

Now even more people were crying.

"Mya, everything lasts for a certain amount of time before it stops working. It's like a pen running out of ink. Or like an old toy that doesn't work anymore."

"Or like Malcolm dying," I said sadly.

"Yes. Eventually people and animals stop working too. Some people grow older and older until their bodies don't work anymore. Then they die. Other people die from being very, very, VERY sick."

"Just like Malcolm."

"Precisely," she said. "When our bodies stop working, we don't get thrown out like empty pens or broken toys. Instead, we are buried in a funeral service, surrounded by everyone who loves us."

"Mr Murphy buried something the other day," I said. "Did he bury Malcolm under the tree?"

Mrs Cherry nodded.

"I understand now," I said. "Malcolm was buried because he's…dead."

That's why Jamar had pointed to the sky. He was really pointing at heaven. Daddy said heaven was way above us, so high we couldn't even get there on a plane.

Hamster heaven. That's where Malcolm was.

"But when we throw out recycling, it gets recycled!" I said. "We could recycle everyone and bring them back, right?"

Mrs Cherry shook her head.

"Mya, when we die, we *never* come back. We can't be recycled." She stopped to think for a moment. "Recycling doesn't bring anything back exactly the same. It changes things, for example, recycled newspaper could be turned into colouring books."

"When we die, we can't come back." I

started sobbing. "So I'll *never* see Malcolm again?"

"We'll *never* see him again," Mrs Cherry said, "but we can *feel* him again."

"What do you mean?" I asked, wiping away my tears.

"It's hard to explain, but I can show you." Mrs Cherry stood up. "Come on, class. We're going outside…"

Chapter 25

It was quiet in the playground. Nobody said anything. Some people were still crying. Others just stood there with puffy, pink eyes.

"Let's go to the tree," Mrs Cherry said. "It's time to say goodbye to Malcolm."

Our class gathered by the tree. There was a tiny daisy beneath it. I remembered Mr Murphy placing it there.

"This is Malcolm's grave," Mrs Cherry said. "A grave is where dead people and animals are buried."

"Will his grave be here forever?" I asked.

"Yes. He will remain here."

It felt strange knowing Malcolm was buried in the ground. He was nearby, but I couldn't stroke or hug or tickle him. I'd never be able to again.

"Whenever you miss him, come to his grave," Mrs Cherry said. "You can talk to him. He won't talk back, but he can feel your presence. He can feel your love for him."

"What happens if we miss him at home?" I asked. "How can we talk to him then?"

"Do you remember what I said earlier about feeling his presence?"

We all nodded.

"When we bury our loved ones, they become one with the earth. Their presence flows into the ground and joins with Mother Nature. Mother Nature controls everything: the wind, the rain and many other things."

I thought it'd be so cool to join with

Mother Nature. I wanted to be the wind and fly around the playground. Or I could be the rain that left puddles to splash in. If I was really lucky, I could be a juicy, green grape.

But I didn't want anyone to eat me!

"Malcolm is buried," Mrs Cherry said. "He is now part of Mother Nature, so that means he's all around us. He's the earth beneath our feet, and the stars in the sky. He's the rain falling from the clouds, and the sand on a golden beach. He's the trees in a forest, and the ocean flowing around the world."

I closed my eyes and felt the sun's warm rays shining on my face. Could Malcolm be the sun too? Was that warm feeling Malcolm's tiny paws touching my skin?

I opened my hands and let the wind rush over my skin. It felt like Malcolm's feet pitter pattering across my palms.

Suddenly the wind rushed around us and picked up a pile of leaves. The leaves blew in a circle, spinning faster and faster until they were a blur. The spinning reminded me of Malcolm running in the hamster wheel.

Mrs Cherry was right. Malcolm was dead, but I could still feel him all around me.

"Class, gather around for a group hug!"

Everyone came together, even Angel and her mean friends.

"Class, I'm so sorry for keeping the truth from you. I should not have lied. I should not have tricked you. Angelo and I are very sorry about that."

Angel grinned when Mrs Cherry said Angelo's name.

"I should have been completely honest with you. Then we could have buried Malcolm together and said our goodbyes." Mrs Cherry wiped her puffy eyes with a tissue. "I regret not telling you the truth before, but it's too late now. What's done is done, what's passed is past."

Mrs Cherry wasn't the only one with regrets. I regretted how naughty I'd been over the past week...

First, I'd gone through other people's bags in class without asking. If someone did that to me, I'd be very angry.

Then I snooped around in the Year Six classroom without asking. If they did that to our class, I would've told them off!

I even went through the school cameras without asking. If Mr Badal did that to me, I would've written to his parents and given him two weeks in detention.

Worst of all, I made Mrs Cherry cry. I didn't want to *ever* make her cry again.

Looking back over the case, everything made sense now.

When Mr Badal said "Get rid" he was telling Mrs Cherry to remove Malcolm's body from the classroom. He didn't want us to be upset when we realised Malcolm was dead.

The dinner lady Mrs Gable looked so scared when I said Malcolm was still around. It was because she knew he was dead.

Mrs Cherry, Mrs Tipple, Mr Badal and Mr Murphy had all been too scared to tell us the truth. They didn't want us to be upset. Well, their plan hadn't worked. Now we were all crying.

I cried because I'd never stroke Malcolm's soft fur again. I cried for not realising he had a really bad cold. Finally, I cried for missing his funeral. At least I could bring pretty flowers to his grave.

I felt better knowing Malcolm was okay. He was dead and he'd never come back, but at least I knew where he was. He wasn't lost. He hadn't been stolen. He was sleeping forever, curled up in a tiny ball.

The bell rang. It was breaktime.

Jamar walked out with his friends. When he saw me, his eyes lit up and he ran over. His friends looked very confused when they saw us together.

"Mya, what's up?" Jamar said. He frowned when he saw my puffy, red eyes. "Did your teacher tell you what happened to Malcolm?"

"He died." I pointed at the sky. "He's up there."

"And there." He pointed at my heart. "He'll always be there."

I blinked back tears, trying not to cry.

"Mya, you're a great friend," Jamar said.

"Me?"

"When Malcolm went missing, you were the only one who looked for him. That sounds like a great friend to me."

"That's what friends are for."

"He was very lucky to have a friend like you. I wish *I* was so lucky…"

"What do you mean?"

"Let's be friends," he said. "I'll be there for you, you be there for me. If you need help with another case, just let me know."

"Okay."

Wow! I couldn't believe it! The Chief Superintendent was my friend! Now I could ask the best police officer for help anytime I liked.

My secret boss would be so jealous when she found out…

"Mya, I'll put in a good word for you, okay?" Jamar said. "You might be Chief Superintendent when you get to Year Six."

"Do you get paid lots of grapes?" I asked, my mouth watering at the thought. "The green ones, not the red ones."

"Um, I prefer money. The first time I got paid, I bought a new badge for only five pounds!"

Five pounds? How expensive! My badge only cost one pound. I didn't tell him that, though. A police officer shouldn't moan about what our things cost. A badge, handcuffs and other stuff were part of the job.

Suddenly Libby rushed over and pointed at the sky. We looked up and saw something fluffy floating down. It landed on my afro hair, so Libby picked it off and gave it to me.

"What is it?" Libby asked.

"White hamster fur," I said. "It looks and feels just like Malcolm's."

Jamar's eyes widened.

"I've seen something like this before," he said. "At my grandad's funeral, a white feather fell from the sky! My mum said it means someone dead is thinking of you."

Instead of a white feather, Malcolm had dropped white fur. It showed he was still thinking of me.

He still loved me.

I felt very sad about losing him, but I started to feel a bit better. He was all around us now. All those times he'd tried to get out of his cage. Now he was free! He could be the trees, the wind, the rain, the snow, the ice, the sand, the sea. Anything and anywhere with anyone.

I looked up to the sky and smiled. I held the hamster fur close to my heart. I'd share the fur with everyone later.

"Malcolm," I whispered, "you were the best school pet in the world. We were very lucky to have you. Wherever you are, I love you very much. Do you still love me?"

A gust of wind tickled my cheeks.

"Good!"

I felt better knowing Malcolm was okay, but something still bothered me…

That something was death.

Death. Just thinking about it was scary.

One day I'd be dead too, and so would my family, friends and everyone else.

All of us. Gone.

Just like Malcolm.

He was dead, but when I remembered him, I felt happy. I remembered him hugging me. I remembered him running in his hamster ball. I remembered his whiskers tickling my hands. We had so many happy memories together! I smiled just thinking of them all.

That's when I realised death wasn't important. Everything we did *before* we died was what really mattered. That's why I remembered Malcolm living, not dying.

When I died, many, many, MANY years in the future, I wanted people to remember all the amazing cases I solved, all the people I helped, and all the bad guys I told off. I wanted people to remember how kind and helpful I was.

When I died, I wanted people to smile, not cry. They'd smile because they remembered all the great things I did. I wouldn't be remembered for dying, I'd be remembered for living.

Just like Malcolm.

And just like you.

CASE CLOSED

Dear Reader

Hello, I hope you enjoyed my book. You can email me at contact@zuniblue.com. I'd love to hear from you!

I'd really appreciate it if you left a book review saying whether you loved it, hated it, or thought it was just okay. It doesn't have to be a long review. Thank you very much!

Keep reading to get your 100 free gifts…

About the Author

Zuni Blue lives in London, England with her parents. She's been writing non-fiction and fiction since she was a kid.

She loves telling stories that show how diverse the world is. Her characters are different races, genders, heights, weights and live with various disabilities and abilities. In Zuni's books, every child is special!

Solve More Cases

Would you like to read another case file?

Mya doesn't share her cases with just anyone, but she knows she can trust you.

Keep reading for more top secret cases she's solved…

The New Boy Who Hears Buzzing

The new boy's ears are buzzing. He must've been bugged, but who did it? Was it a student? A teacher? Or some bad guys?

To solve the mystery, Detective Dove must face the detention kids, a crafty inspector, and some naughty officers at the police station...

The Parents With A Sleepover Secret

Mya has to stay at her enemy Angel's house. Angel is forcing her to solve a tough case. If the case isn't solved, Mya will be kicked off the Children's Police Force!

To solve the mystery, Detective Dove must face an angry poodle, a scary garage, and the meanest girl in the universe...

The Fat Girl Who Never Eats

Ten school burgers were stolen. Everyone blames the fat girl, but no one saw her do it. Is she the burger thief or is it someone else?

To solve the mystery, Detective Dove must face her crafty dad, a strange caretaker, and the shocking secret in the school basement...

The Mean Girl Who Never Speaks

There's a new girl at school. She never speaks, never smiles and never plays with other kids. Does that mean she's mean? Maybe. Maybe not...

To solve the mystery, Detective Dove must face a suspicious teacher, the school bully, and the meanest boss in the world...

Dedications

This book is dedicated to everyone whose pet has gone missing or passed away.

Thank you to my family and friends. I appreciate all the love and support you have given me. I couldn't have done this without you.

An extra special thank you to every reader who's emailed me. I love hearing from you!

100 Free Gifts For You

There are 100 FREE printables waiting for you!

Certificates, bookmarks, wallpapers and more! You can choose your favourite colour: red, yellow, pink, green, orange, purple or blue.

You don't need money or an email address. Check out www.zuniblue.com to print your free gifts today.

Made in the USA
Monee, IL
28 September 2020

43466950R00157